Penguin Bo

D1434105

Decline of the English Murder
and Other Essays

George Orwell (whose real name was Eric Blair)
was born in India in 1903, and was educated
at Eton. From 1922 to 1928 he served in Burma
in the Indian Imperial Police. For the next two
years he lived in Paris, and then came to England
as a schoolteacher. Later he worked in a
book-shop. In 1937 he went to Spain to fight for
the Republicans and was wounded. During the
Second World War he was a member of the
Home Guard and worked for the B.B.C. In
1943 he joined the staff of *Tribune*, contributing
a regular page of political and literary
commentary, *As I Please*. He later became a
regular contributor to the *Observer*, for which
newspaper he went as a special correspondent to
France and Germany. He died in London in
1950.

His publications include *Down and Out in Paris
and London, Burmese Days, The Road to Wigan
Pier, Coming Up For Air, Keep the Aspidistra
Flying, Homage to Catalonia*, and *Inside the
Whale*. Orwell's name became widely known
with the publication, in 1945, of *Animal Farm*,
which has sold more than a million copies.
Nineteen Eighty-Four had a similar success, and
aroused extraordinary interest as a film and on
television.

Decline of the English Murder

and other essays

George Orwell

Penguin Books
in association with Secker & Warburg

Penguin Books Ltd, Harmondsworth,
Middlesex, England
Penguin Books Pty Ltd, Ringwood,
Victoria, Australia

This selection first published in Penguin Books
1965

Copyright © Estate of Eric Blair, 1946, 1931,
1946, 1950, 1944, 1942, 1944, 1940, 1941, 1946,
1945, 1947, 1953

Made and printed in Great Britain by
C. Nicholls and Company Ltd

Set in Linotype Granjon

Contents

Bibliographical Note

'Decline of the English Murder' first appeared in *Tribune* (1946), 'A Hanging' in *Adelphi* (August 1931), and 'How the Poor Die' in *Now* (November 1946). All three essays were included in the selection *Shooting an Elephant* (1950).

'Benefit of Clergy' was withdrawn from *The Saturday Book for 1944*, 'Rudyard Kipling' first appeared in *Horizon* (February 1942), 'Raffles and Miss Blandish' in *Horizon* (October 1944), 'Charles Dickens' in the book *Inside the Whale* (1940), and 'The Art of Donald McGill' in *Horizon* (September 1941). These five essays were included in the selection *Critical Essays* (1946).

'Notes on Nationalism' first appeared in *Polemic* (October 1945), and 'Why I Write' in *Gangrel* (1947). These two essays appeared in the selection *Such, Such Were the Joys* (1953).

Decline of the English Murder

It is Sunday afternoon, preferably before the war. The wife is already asleep in the armchair, and the children have been sent out for a nice long walk. You put your feet up on the sofa, settle your spectacles on your nose, and open the *News of the World*. Roast beef and Yorkshire, or roast pork and apple sauce, followed up by suet pudding and driven home, as it were, by a cup of mahogany-brown tea, have put you in just the right mood. Your pipe is drawing sweetly, the sofa cushions are soft underneath you, the fire is well alight, the air is warm and stagnant. In these blissful circumstances, what is it that you want to read about?

Naturally, about a murder. But what kind of murder? If one examines the murders which have given the greatest amount of pleasure to the British public, the murders whose story is known in its general outline to almost everyone and which have been made into novels and re-hashed over and over again by the Sunday papers, one finds a fairly strong family resemblance running through the greater number of them. Our great period in murder, our Elizabethan period, so to speak, seems to have been between roughly 1850 and 1925, and the murderers whose reputation has stood the test of time are the following: Dr Palmer of Rugeley, Jack the Ripper, Neill Cream, Mrs Maybrick, Dr Crippen, Seddon, Joseph Smith, Armstrong, and Bywaters and Thompson. In addition, in 1919 or thereabouts, there was another very celebrated case which fits into the general pattern but which I had better not mention by name, because the accused man was acquitted.

Of the above-mentioned nine cases, at least four have had successful novels based on them, one has been made into a popular melodrama, and the amount of literature surrounding them, in the form of newspaper write-ups, criminological treatises and reminiscences by lawyers and police officers, would make a considerable library. It is difficult to believe that any recent English crime will be remembered so long and so intimately, and not only because the violence of external events has made murder seem unimportant, but because the prevalent type of crime seems to be changing. The principal *cause célèbre* of the war years was the so-called Cleft Chin Murder, which has now been written up in a popular booklet;* the verbatim account of the trial was published some time last year by Messrs Jarrolds with an introduction by Mr Bechhofer Roberts. Before returning to this pitiful and sordid case, which is only interesting from a sociological and perhaps a legal point of view, let me try to define what it is that the readers of Sunday papers mean when they say fretfully that 'you never seem to get a good murder nowadays'.

In considering the nine murders I named above, one can start by excluding the Jack the Ripper case, which is in a class by itself. Of the other eight, six were poisoning cases, and eight of the ten criminals belonged to the middle class. In one way or another, sex was a powerful motive in all but two cases, and in at least four cases respectability – the desire to gain a secure position in life, or not to forfeit one's social position by some scandal such as a divorce – was one of the main reasons for committing murder. In more than half the cases, the object was to get hold of a certain known sum of money such as a legacy or an insurance policy, but the amount involved was nearly always small. In most of the

* *The Cleft Chin Murder*, by R. Alwyn Raymond (Claude Morris, 1s. 6d.)

cases the crime only came to light slowly, as the result of careful investigations which started off with the suspicions of neighbours or relatives; and in nearly every case there was some dramatic coincidence, in which the finger of Providence could be clearly seen, or one of those episodes that no novelist would dare to make up, such as Crippen's flight across the Atlantic with his mistress dressed as a boy, or Joseph Smith playing 'Nearer, my God, to Thee' on the harmonium while one of his wives was drowning in the next room. The background of all these crimes, except Neill Cream's, was essentially domestic; of twelve victims, seven were either wife or husband of the murderer.

With all this in mind one can construct what would be, from a *News of the World* reader's point of view, the 'perfect' murder. The murderer should be a little man of the professional class – a dentist or a solicitor, say – living an intensely respectable life somewhere in the suburbs, and preferably in a semi-detached house, which will allow the neighbours to hear suspicious sounds through the wall. He should be either chairman of the local Conservative Party branch, or a leading Nonconformist and strong Temperance advocate. He should go astray through cherishing a guilty passion for his secretary or the wife of a rival professional man, and should only bring himself to the point of murder after long and terrible wrestles with his conscience. Having decided on murder, he should plan it all with the utmost cunning, and only slip up over some tiny unforeseeable detail. The means chosen should, of course, be poison. In the last analysis he should commit murder because this seems to him less disgraceful, and less damaging to his career, than being detected in adultery. With this kind of background, a crime can have dramatic and even tragic qualities which make it memorable and excite pity for both victim and murderer. Most of the crimes mentioned above have a touch of this atmosphere, and in three cases, including the one I referred to but did not name, the story approximates to the one I have outlined.

Now compare the Cleft Chin Murder. There is no depth of feeling in it. It was almost chance that the two people concerned committed that particular murder, and it was only by good luck that they did not commit several others. The background was not domesticity, but the anonymous life of the dance-halls and the false values of the American film. The two culprits were an eighteen-year-old ex-waitress named Elizabeth Jones, and an American army deserter, posing as an officer, named Karl Hulten. They were only together for six days, and it seems doubtful whether, until they were arrested, they even learned one another's true names. They met casually in a teashop, and that night went out for a ride in a stolen army truck. Jones described herself as a strip-tease artist, which was not strictly true (she had given one unsuccessful performance in this line), and declared that she wanted to do something dangerous, 'like being a gun-moll'. Hulten described himself as a big-time Chicago gangster, which was also untrue. They met a girl bicycling along the road, and to show how tough he was Hulten ran over her with his truck, after which the pair robbed her of the few shillings that were on her. On another occasion they knocked out a girl to whom they had offered a lift, took her coat and handbag and threw her into a river. Finally, in the most wanton way, they murdered a taxi-driver who happened to have £8 in his pocket. Soon afterwards they parted. Hulten was caught because he had foolishly kept the dead man's car, and Jones made spontaneous confessions to the police. In court each prisoner incriminated the other. In between crimes, both of them seem to have behaved with the utmost callousness : they spent the dead taxi-driver's £8 at the dog races.

Judging from her letters, the girl's case has a certain amount of psychological interest, but this murder probably captured the headlines because it provided distraction amid the doodle-bugs and the anxieties of the Battle of France. Jones and Hulten committed their murder to the tune of V1, and were convicted to the tune of V2. There was also considerable excitement because – as has become usual in England – the man was sentenced to death and the girl to imprisonment. According to Mr Raymond, the reprieving of Jones caused widespread indignation and streams of telegrams to the Home Secretary: in her native town, 'SHE SHOULD HANG' was chalked on the walls beside pictures of a figure dangling from a gallows. Considering that only ten women have been hanged in Britain this century, and that the practice has gone out largely because of popular feeling against it, it is difficult not to feel that this clamour to hang an eighteen-year-old girl was due partly to the brutalizing effects of war. Indeed, the whole meaningless story, with its atmosphere of dance-halls, movie-palaces, cheap perfume, false names and stolen cars, belongs essentially to a war period.

Perhaps it is significant that the most talked-of English murder of recent years should have been committed by an American and an English girl who had become partly Americanized. But it is difficult to believe that this case will be so long remembered as the old domestic poisoning dramas, product of a stable society where the all-prevailing hypocrisy did at least ensure that crimes as serious as murder should have strong emotions behind them.

1946

A Hanging

It was in Burma, a sodden morning of the rains. A sickly light, like yellow tinfoil, was slanting over the high walls into the jail yard. We were waiting outside the condemned cells, a row of sheds fronted with double bars, like small animal cages. Each cell measured about ten feet by ten and was quite bare within except for a plank bed and a pot for drinking water. In some of them brown, silent men were squatting at the inner bars, with their blankets draped round them. These were the condemned men, due to be hanged within the next week or two.

One prisoner had been brought out of his cell. He was a Hindu, a puny wisp of a man, with a shaven head and vague liquid eyes. He had a thick, sprouting moustache, absurdly too big for his body, rather like the moustache of a comic man on the films. Six tall Indian warders were guarding him and getting him ready for the gallows. Two of them stood by with rifles and fixed bayonets, while the others handcuffed him, passed a chain through his handcuffs and fixed it to their belts, and lashed his arms tight to his sides. They crowded very close about him, with their hands always on him in a careful, caressing grip, as though all the while feeling him to make sure he was there. It was like men handling a fish which is still alive and may jump back into the water. But he stood quite unresisting, yielding his arms limply to the ropes, as though he hardly noticed what was happening.

Eight o'clock struck and a bugle call, desolately thin in the

wet air, floated from the distant barracks. The superintendent of the jail, who was standing apart from the rest of us,
moodily prodding the gravel with his stick, raised his head
at the sound. He was an army doctor, with a grey tooth-
brush moustache and a gruff voice. 'For God's sake hurry
up, Francis,' he said irritably. 'The man ought to have been
dead by this time. Aren't you ready yet?'

Francis, the head jailer, a fat Dravidian in a white drill
suit and gold spectacles, waved his black hand. 'Yes sir, yes
sir,' he bubbled. 'All iss satisfactorily prepared. The hangman iss waiting. We shall proceed.'

'Well, quick march, then. The prisoners can't get their
breakfast till this job's over.'

We set out for the gallows. Two warders marched on
either side of the prisoner, with their rifles at the slope; two
others marched close against him, gripping him by arm
and shoulder, as though at once pushing and supporting
him. The rest of us, magistrates and the like, followed behind. Suddenly, when we had gone ten yards, the procession
stopped short without any order or warning. A dreadful
thing had happened – a dog, come goodness knows whence,
had appeared in the yard. It came bounding among us with
a loud volley of barks and leapt round us wagging its whole
body, wild with glee at finding so many human beings together. It was a large woolly dog, half Airedale, half pariah.
For a moment it pranced round us, and then, before anyone
could stop it, it had made a dash for the prisoner, and
jumping up tried to lick his face. Everybody stood aghast,
too taken aback even to grab the dog.

'Who let that bloody brute in here?' said the superintendent angrily. 'Catch it, someone!'

A warder, detached from the escort, charged clumsily after
the dog, but it danced and gambolled just out of his reach,
taking everything as part of the game. A young Eurasian

jailer picked up a handful of gravel and tried to stone the dog away, but it dodged the stones and came after us again. Its yaps echoed from the jail walls. The prisoner, in the grasp of the two warders, looked on incuriously, as though this was another formality of the hanging. It was several minutes before someone managed to catch the dog. Then we put my handkerchief through its collar and moved off once more, with the dog still straining and whimpering.

It was about forty yards to the gallows. I watched the bare brown back of the prisoner marching in front of me. He walked clumsily with his bound arms, but quite steadily, with that bobbing gait of the Indian who never straightens his knees. At each step his muscles slid neatly into place, the lock of hair on his scalp danced up and down, his feet printed themselves on the wet gravel. And once, in spite of the men who gripped him by each shoulder, he stepped slightly aside to avoid a puddle on the path.

It is curious, but till that moment I had never realized what it means to destroy a healthy, conscious man. When I saw the prisoner step aside to avoid the puddle I saw the mystery, the unspeakable wrongness, of cutting a life short when it is in full tide. This man was not dying, he was alive just as we are alive. All the organs of his body were working – bowels digesting food, skin renewing itself, nails growing, tissues forming – all toiling away in solemn foolery. His nails would still be growing when he stood on the drop, when he was falling through the air with a tenth of a second to live. His eyes saw the yellow gravel and the grey walls, and his brain still remembered, foresaw, reasoned – even about puddles. He and we were a party of men walking together, seeing, hearing, feeling, understanding the same world; and in two minutes, with a sudden snap, one of us would be gone – one mind less, one world less.

The gallows stood in a small yard, separate from the main

grounds of the prison, and overgrown with tall prickly weeds. It was a brick erection like three sides of a shed, with planking on top, and above that two beams and a crossbar with the rope dangling. The hangman, a grey-haired convict in the white uniform of the prison, was waiting beside his machine. He greeted us with a servile crouch as we entered. At a word from Francis the two warders, gripping the prisoner more closely than ever, half led, half pushed him to the gallows and helped him clumsily up the ladder. Then the hangman climbed up and fixed the rope round the prisoner's neck.

We stood waiting, five yards away. The warders had formed in a rough circle round the gallows. And then, when the noose was fixed, the prisoner began crying out to his god. It was a high, reiterated cry of 'Ram! Ram! Ram! Ram!' not urgent and fearful like a prayer or cry for help, but steady, rhythmical, almost like the tolling of a bell. The dog answered the sound with a whine. The hangman, still standing on the gallows, produced a small cotton bag like a flour sack and drew it down over the prisoner's face. But the sound, muffled by the cloth, still persisted, over and over again: 'Ram! Ram! Ram! Ram! Ram!'

The hangman climbed down and stood ready, holding the lever. Minutes seemed to pass. The steady, muffled crying from the prisoner went on and on, 'Ram! Ram! Ram!' never faltering for an instant. The superintendent, his head on his chest, was slowly poking the ground with his stick; perhaps he was counting the cries, allowing the prisoner a fixed number – fifty, perhaps, or a hundred. Everyone had changed colour. The Indians had gone grey like bad coffee, and one or two of the bayonets were wavering. We looked at the lashed, hooded man on the drop, and listened to his cries – each cry another second of life; the same thought was in all our minds: oh, kill him quickly, get it over, stop that abominable noise!

Suddenly the superintendent made up his mind. Throwing up his head he made a swift motion with his stick. 'Chalo!' he shouted almost fiercely.

There was a clanking noise, and then dead silence. The prisoner had vanished, and the rope was twisting on itself. I let go of the dog, and it galloped immediately to the back of the gallows; but when it got there it stopped short, barked, and then retreated into a corner of the yard, where it stood among the weeds, looking timorously out at us. We went round the gallows to inspect the prisoner's body. He was dangling with his toes pointed straight downwards, very slowly revolving, as dead as a stone.

The superintendent reached out with his stick and poked the bare brown body; it oscillated slightly. '*He*'s all right,' said the superintendent. He backed out from under the gallows, and blew out a deep breath. The moody look had gone out of his face quite suddenly. He glanced at his wrist-watch. 'Eight minutes past eight. Well, that's all for this morning, thank God.'

The warders unfixed bayonets and marched away. The dog, sobered and conscious of having misbehaved itself, slipped after them. We walked out of the gallows yard, past the condemned cells with their waiting prisoners, into the big central yard of the prison. The convicts, under the command of warders armed with lathis, were already receiving their breakfast. They squatted in long rows, each man holding a tin pannikin, while two warders with buckets marched round ladling out rice; it seemed quite a homely, jolly scene, after the hanging. An enormous relief had come upon us now that the job was done. One felt an impulse to sing, to break into a run, to snigger. All at once everyone began chattering gaily.

The Eurasian boy walking beside me nodded towards the way we had come, with a knowing smile: 'Do you know, sir, our friend (he meant the dead man) when he heard his appeal had been dismissed, he pissed on the floor of his cell. From fright. Kindly take one of my cigarettes, sir. Do you not admire my new silver case, sir? From the box wallah, two rupees eight annas. Classy European style.'

Several people laughed – at what, nobody seemed certain.

Francis was walking by the superintendent, talking garrulously : 'Well, sir, all hass passed off with the utmost satisfactoriness. It was all finished – flick! like that. It iss not always so – oah, no! I have known cases where the doctor wass obliged to go beneath the gallows and pull the prissoner's legs to ensure decease. Most disagreeable!'

'Wriggling about, eh? That's bad,' said the superintendent.

'Ach, sir, it iss worse when they become refractory! One man, I recall, clung to the bars of hiss cage when we went to take him out. You will scarcely credit, sir, that it took six warders to dislodge him, three pulling at each leg. We reasoned with him. "My dear fellow," we said, "think of all the pain and trouble you are causing to us!" But no, he would not listen! Ach, he wass very troublesome!'

I found that I was laughing quite loudly. Everyone was laughing. Even the superintendent grinned in a tolerant way. 'You'd better all come out and have a drink,' he said quite genially. 'I've got a bottle of whisky in the car. We could do with it.'

We went through the big double gates of the prison into the road. 'Pulling at his legs!' exclaimed a Burmese magistrate suddenly, and burst into a loud chuckling. We all began laughing again. At that moment Francis's anecdote seemed extraordinarily funny. We all had a drink together, native and European alike, quite amicably. The dead man was a hundred yards away.

Benefit of Clergy
Some Notes on Salvador Dali

Autobiography is only to be trusted when it reveals something disgraceful. A man who gives a good account of himself is probably lying, since any life when viewed from the inside is simply a series of defeats. However, even the most flagrantly dishonest book (Frank Harris's autobiographical writings are an example) can without intending it give a truer picture of its author. Dali's recently published *Life** comes under this heading. Some of the incidents in it are flatly incredible, others have been rearranged and romanticized, and not merely the humiliation but the persistent *ordinariness* of everyday life been cut out. Dali is even by his own diagnosis narcissistic, and his autobiography is simply a strip-tease act conducted in pink limelight. But as a record of fantasy, of the perversion of instinct that has been made possible by the machine age, it has great value.

Here, then, are some of the episodes in Dali's life from his earliest years onward. Which of them are true and which are imaginary hardly matters: the point is that this is the kind of thing that Dali would have *liked* to do.

When he is six years old there is some excitement over the appearance of Halley's comet:

Suddenly one of my father's office clerks appeared in the drawing-room doorway and announced that the comet could be seen from the terrace. . . . While crossing the hall I caught sight of my little three-year-old sister crawling unobtrusively

* *The Secret Life of Salvador Dali* (Dial Press, New York).

through a doorway. I stopped, hesitated a second, then gave her a terrible kick in the head, as though it had been a ball, and continued running, carried away with a 'delirious joy' induced by this savage act. But my father, who was behind me, caught me and led me down into his office, where I remained as a punishment till dinner-time.

A year earlier than this Dali had 'suddenly, as most of my ideas occur', flung another little boy off a suspension bridge. Several other incidents of the same kind are recorded, including (this was when he was twenty-nine years old) knocking down and trampling on a girl 'until they had to tear her, bleeding out of my reach'.

When he is about five he gets hold of a wounded bat which he puts into a tin pail. Next morning he finds that the bat is almost dead and is covered with ants which are devouring it. He puts it in his mouth, ants and all, and bites it almost in half.

When he is adolescent a girl falls desperately in love with him. He kisses and caresses her so as to excite her as much as possible, but refuses to go further. He resolves to keep this up for five years (he calls it his 'five-year plan'), enjoying her humiliation and the sense of power it gives him. He frequently tells her that at the end of five years he will desert her, and when the time comes he does so.

Till well into adult life he keeps up the practice of masturbation, and likes to do this, apparently, in front of a looking-glass. For ordinary purposes he is impotent, it appears, till the age of thirty or so. When he first meets his future wife, Gala, he is greatly tempted to push her off a precipice. He is aware that there is something that she wants him to do to her, and after their first kiss the confession is made :

I threw back Gala's head, pulling it by the hair, and trembling with complete hysteria, I commanded :
'Now tell me what you want me to do with you! But tell me

slowly, looking me in the eye, with the crudest, the most fero-
ciously erotic words that can make both of us feel the greatest
shame !'

... Then Gala, transforming the last glimmer of her expression of pleasure into the hard light of her own tyranny, answered:

'I want you to kill me !'

He is somewhat disappointed by this demand, since it is
merely what he wanted to do already. He contemplates
throwing her off the bell-tower of the Cathedral of Toledo,
but refrains from doing so.

During the Spanish Civil War he astutely avoids taking
sides, and makes a trip to Italy. He feels himself more and
more drawn towards the aristocracy, frequents smart *salons*,
finds himself wealthy patrons, and is photographed with
the plump Vicomte de Noailles, whom he describes as his
'Mæcenas'. When the European War approaches he has
one preoccupation only : how to find a place which has good
cookery and from which he can make a quick bolt if danger
comes too near. He fixes on Bordeaux, and duly flees to Spain
during the Battle of France. He stays in Spain long enough
to pick up a few anti-red atrocity stories, then makes for
America. The story ends in a blaze of respectability. Dali, at
thirty-seven, has become a devoted husband, is cured of his
aberrations, or some of them, and is completely reconciled
to the Catholic Church. He is also, one gathers, making a
good deal of money.

However, he has by no means ceased to take pride in the
pictures of his Surrealist period, with titles like 'The Great
Masturbator', 'Sodomy of a Skull with a Grand Piano', etc.
There are reproductions of these all the way through the
book. Many of Dali's drawings are simply representational
and have a characteristic to be noted later. But from his
Surrealist paintings and photographs the two things that

stand out are sexual perversity and necrophilia. Sexual objects and symbols – some of them well known, like our old friend the high-heeled slipper, others, like the crutch and the cup of warm milk, patented by Dali himself – recur over and over again, and there is a fairly well-marked excretory motif as well. In his painting, 'Le Jeu Lugubre', he says, 'the drawers bespattered with excrement were painted with such minute and realistic complacency that the whole little Surrealist group was anguished by the question: Is he coprophagic or not?' Dali adds firmly that he is *not*, and that he regards this aberration as 'repulsive', but it seems to be only at that point that his interest in excrement stops. Even when he recounts the experience of watching a woman urinate standing up, he has to add the detail that she misses her aim and dirties her shoes. It is not given to any one person to have all the vices, and Dali also boasts that he is not homosexual, but otherwise he seems to have as good an outfit of perversions as anyone could wish for.

However, his most notable characteristic is his necrophilia. He himself freely admits to this, and claims to have been cured of it. Dead faces, skulls, corpses of animals occur fairly frequently in his pictures, and the ants which devoured the dying bat make countless reappearances. One photograph shows an exhumed corpse, far gone in decomposition. Another shows the dead donkeys putrefying on top of grand pianos which formed part of the Surrealist film, *Le Chien Andalou*. Dali still looks back on these donkeys with great enthusiasm.

I 'made up' the putrefaction of the donkeys with great pots of sticky glue which I poured over them. Also I emptied their eye-sockets and made them larger by hacking them out with scissors. In the same way I furiously cut their mouths open to make the rows of their teeth show to better advantage, and I added several jaws to each mouth, so that it would appear that although the donkeys were already rotting they were vomiting up a little more of their own death, above those other rows of teeth formed by the keys of the black pianos.

And finally there is the picture – apparently some kind of faked photograph – of 'Mannequin Rotting in a Taxi-cab'. Over the already somewhat bloated face and breast of an apparently dead girl, huge snails are crawling. In the caption below the picture Dali notes that these are Burgundy snails – that is, the edible kind.

Of course, in this long book of 400 quarto pages there is more than I have indicated, but I do not think that I have given an unfair account of its moral atmosphere and mental scenery. It is a book that stinks. If it were possible for a book to give a physical stink off its pages, this one would – a thought that might please Dali, who before wooing his future wife for the first time rubbed himself all over with an ointment made of goat's dung boiled up in fish glue. But against this has to be set the fact that Dali is a draughtsman of very exceptional gifts. He is also, to judge by the minuteness and the sureness of his drawing, a very hard worker. He is an exhibitionist and a careerist, but he is not a fraud. He has fifty times more talent than most of the people who would denounce his morals and peer at his paintings. And the two sets of facts, taken together, raise a question which for lack of any basis of agreement seldom gets a real discussion.

The point is that you have here a direct, unmistakable assault on sanity and decency; and even – since some of Dali's pictures would tend to poison the imagination like a pornographic post card – on life itself. What Dali has done and what he has imagined is debatable, but in his outlook, his character, the bedrock decency of a human being does not exist. He is as anti-social as a flea. Clearly such people are undesirable, and a society in which they can flourish has something wrong with it.

Now, if you showed this book, with its illustrations, to Lord Elton, to Mr Alfred Noyes, to *The Times* leader-writers who exult over the 'eclipse of the highbrow' – in fact, to any 'sensible' art-hating English person – it is easy to imagine what kind of response you would get. They would flatly refuse to see any merit in Dali whatever. Such people are not only unable to admit that what is morally degraded can be aesthetically right, but their real demand of every artist is that he shall pat them on the back and tell them that thought is unnecessary. And they can be especially dangerous at a time like the present, when the Ministry of Information and the British Council put power into their hands. For their impulse is not only to crush every new talent as it appears, but to castrate the past as well. Witness the renewed highbrow-baiting that is now going on in this country and America, with its outcry not only against Joyce, Proust and Lawrence, but even against T. S. Eliot.

But if you talk to the kind of person who *can* see Dali's merits, the response that you get is not as a rule very much better. If you say that Dali, though a brilliant draughtsman, is a dirty little scoundrel, you are looked upon as a savage. If you say that you don't like rotting corpses, and that people who do like rotting corpses are mentally diseased, it is assumed that you lack the aesthetic sense. Since 'Mannequin Rotting in a Taxi-cab' is a good composition (as it undoubtedly is), it cannot be a disgusting, degrading picture; whereas Noyes, Elton, etc., would tell you that because it is disgusting it cannot be a good composition. And between these two fallacies there is no middle position; or, rather, there is a middle position, but we seldom hear much about it. On the one side *Kulturbolschevismus*: on the other (though the phrase itself is out of fashion) 'Art for Art's sake'. Obscenity is a very difficult question to discuss honestly. People are too frightened either of seeming to be shocked or of seeming not to be shocked, to be able to define the relationship between art and morals.

It will be seen that what the defenders of Dali are claiming is a kind of *benefit of clergy*. The artist is to be exempt from the moral laws that are binding on ordinary people. Just pronounce the magic word 'Art', and everything is O.K. Rotting corpses with snails crawling over them are O.K.; kicking little girls on the head is O.K.; even a film like *L'Âge d'Or* is O.K.* It is also O.K. that Dali should batten on France for years and then scuttle off like a rat as soon as France is in danger. So long as you can paint well enough to pass the test, all shall be forgiven you.

One can see how false this is if one extends it to cover ordinary crime. In an age like our own, when the artist is an altogether exceptional person, he must be allowed a certain amount of irresponsibility, just as a pregnant woman is. Still, no one would say that a pregnant woman should be allowed to commit murder, nor would anyone make such a claim for the artist, however gifted. If Shakespeare returned to the earth tomorrow, and if it were found that his favourite recreation was raping little girls in railway carriages, we should not tell him to go ahead with it on the ground that he might write another *King Lear*. And, after all, the worst crimes are not always the punishable ones. By encouraging necrophilic reveries one probably does quite as much harm as by, say, picking pockets at the races. One ought to be able to hold in one's head simultaneously the two facts that Dali is a good draughtsman and a disgusting human being. The one does not invalidate or, in a sense, affect the other. The first thing that we demand of a wall is

* Dali mentions *L'Âge d'Or* and adds that its first public showing was broken up by hooligans, but he does not say in detail what it was about. According to Henry Miller's account of it, it showed among other things some fairly detailed shots of a woman defecating.

that it shall stand up. If it stands up, it is a good wall, and the question of what purpose it serves is separable from that. And yet even the best wall in the world deserves to be pulled down if it surrounds a concentration camp. In the same way it should be possible to say, 'This is a good book or a good picture, and it ought to be burned by the public hangman.' Unless one can say that, at least in imagination, one is shrinking the implications of the fact that an artist is also a citizen and a human being.

Not, of course, that Dali's autobiography, or his pictures, ought to be suppressed. Short of the dirty post cards that used to be sold in Mediterranean seaport towns, it is doubtful policy to suppress anything, and Dali's fantasies probably cast useful light on the decay of capitalist civilization. But what he clearly needs is diagnosis. The question is not so much *what* he is as *why* he is like that. It ought not to be in doubt that he is a diseased intelligence, probably not much altered by his alleged conversion, since genuine penitents, or people who have returned to sanity, do not flaunt their past vices in that complacent way. He is a symptom of the world's illness. The important thing is not to denounce him as a cad who ought to be horsewhipped, or to defend him as a genius who ought not to be questioned, but to find out *why* he exhibits that particular set of aberrations.

The answer is probably discoverable in his pictures, and those I myself am not competent to examine. But I can point to one clue which perhaps takes one part of the distance. This is the old-fashioned, over-ornate, Edwardian style of drawing to which Dali tends to revert when he is not being Surrealist. Some of Dali's drawings are reminiscent of Dürer : one (p. 113) seems to show the influence of Beardsley, another (p. 269) seems to borrow something from Blake. But the most persistent strain is the Edwardian one. When

I opened the book for the first time and looked at its innumerable marginal illustrations, I was haunted by a resemblance which I could not immediately pin down. I fetched up at the ornamental candlestick at the beginning of Part I (p. 7). What did this remind me of? Finally I tracked it down. It reminded me of a large, vulgar, expensively got-up edition of Anatole France (in translation) which must have been published about 1914. That had ornamental chapter headings and tail pieces after this style. Dali's candlestick displays at one end a curly fish-like creature that looks curiously familiar (it seems to be based on the conventional dolphin), and at the other is the burning candle. This candle, which recurs in one picture after another, is a very old friend. You will find it, with the same picturesque gouts of wax arranged on its sides, in those phoney electric lights done up as candlesticks which are popular in sham-Tudor country hotels. This candle, and the design beneath it, convey at once an intense feeling of sentimentality. As though to counteract this, Dali has spattered a quill-full of ink all over the page, but without avail. The same impression keeps popping up on page after page. The design at the bottom of page 62, for instance, would nearly go into *Peter Pan*. The figure on page 224, in spite of having her cranium elongated into an immense sausage-like shape, is the witch of the fairy-tale books. The horse on page 234 and the unicorn on page 218 might be illustrations to James Branch Cabell. The rather pansified drawings of youths on pages 97, 100 and elsewhere convey the same impression. Picturesqueness keeps breaking in. Take away the skulls, ants, lobsters, telephones and other paraphernalia, and every now and again you are back in the world of Barrie, Rackham, Dunsany and *Where the Rainbow Ends*.

Curiously enough, some of the naughty-naughty touches in Dali's autobiography tie up with the same period. When

I read the passage I quoted at the beginning, about the kicking of the little sister's head, I was aware of another phantom resemblance. What was it ? Of course ! *Ruthless Rhymes for Heartless Homes*, by Harry Graham. Such rhymes were very popular round about 1912, and one that ran :

> Poor little Willy is crying so sore,
> A sad little boy is he,
> For he's broken his little sister's neck
> And he'll have no jam for tea,

might almost have been founded on Dali's anecdote. Dali, of course, is aware of his Edwardian leanings, and makes capital out of them, more or less in a spirit of pastiche. He professes an especial affection for the year 1900, and claims that every ornamental object of 1900 is full of mystery, poetry, eroticism, madness, perversity, etc. Pastiche, however, usually implies a real affection for the thing parodied. It seems to be, if not the rule, at any rate distinctly common for an intellectual bent to be accompanied by a non-rational, even childish urge in the same direction. A sculptor, for instance, is interested in planes and curves, but he is also a person who enjoys the physical act of mucking about with clay or stone. An engineer is a person who enjoys the feel of tools, the noise of dynamos and the smell of oil. A psychiatrist usually has a leaning towards some sexual aberration himself. Darwin became a biologist partly because he was a country gentleman and fond of animals. It may be, therefore, that Dali's seemingly perverse cult of Edwardian things (for example, his 'discovery' of the 1900 subway entrances) is merely the symptom of a much deeper, less conscious affection. The innumerable, beautifully executed copies of text-book illustrations, solemnly labelled *le rossignol, une montre* and so on, which he scatters all over his margins, may be meant partly as a joke. The little boy in knickerbockers playing with a diabolo on page 103 is a perfect period piece. But perhaps these things are also there because Dali can't help drawing that kind of thing, because it is to that period and that style of drawing that he really belongs.

If so, his aberrations are partly explicable. Perhaps they are a way of assuring himself that he is not commonplace. The two qualities that Dali unquestionably possesses are a gift for drawing and an atrocious egoism. 'At seven,' he says in the first paragraph of his book, 'I wanted to be Napoleon. And my ambition has been growing steadily ever since.' This is worded in a deliberately startling way, but no doubt it is substantially true. Such feelings are common enough. 'I knew I was a genius', somebody said once to me, 'long before I knew what I was going to be a genius *about*.' And suppose that you have nothing in you except your egoism and a dexterity that goes no higher than the elbow; suppose that your real gift is for a detailed, academic, representational style of drawing, your real *métier* to be an illustrator of scientific text-books. How then do you become Napoleon ?

There is always one escape : *into wickedness*. Always do the thing that will shock and wound people. At five, throw a little boy off a bridge, strike an old doctor across the face with a whip and break his spectacles – or, at any rate, dream about doing such things. Twenty years later, gouge the eyes out of dead donkeys with a pair of scissors. Along those lines you can always feel yourself original. And after all, it pays! It is much less dangerous than crime. Making all allowance for the probable suppressions in Dali's autobiography, it is clear that he has not had to suffer for his eccentricities as he would have done in an earlier age. He grew up into the corrupt world of the nineteen-twenties, when sophistication was immensely widespread and every European capital swarmed with aristocrats and rentiers who had given up sport and politics and taken to patronizing the arts. If you threw dead donkeys at people, they threw money back. A phobia for grasshoppers – which a few decades back would merely have provoked a snigger – was now an interesting 'complex' which could be profitably exploited. And when that particular world collapsed before the German Army, America was waiting. You could even top it all up with religious conversion, moving at one hop and without a shadow of repentance from the fashionable *salons* of Paris to Abraham's bosom.

That, perhaps, is the essential outline of Dali's history. But, why his aberrations should be the particular ones they were, and why it should be so easy to 'sell' such horrors as rotting corpses to a sophisticated public – those are questions for the psychologist and the sociological critic. Marxist criticism has a short way with such phenomena as Surrealism. They are 'bourgeois decadence' (much play is made with the phrases 'corpse poisons' and 'decaying rentier class'), and that is that. But though this probably states a fact, it does not establish a connexion. One would still like to know *why* Dali's leaning was towards necrophilia (and not, say, homosexuality), and *why* the rentiers and the aristocrats should buy his pictures instead of hunting and making love like their grandfathers. Mere moral disapproval does not get one any further. But neither ought one to pretend, in the name of 'detachment', that such pictures as 'Mannequin Rotting in a Taxi-cab' are morally neutral. They are diseased and disgusting, and any investigation ought to start out from that fact.

1944

How the Poor Die

In the year 1929 I spent several weeks in the Hôpital X, in the fifteenth arrondissement of Paris. The clerks put me through the usual third-degree at the reception desk, and indeed I was kept answering questions for some twenty minutes before they would let me in. If you have ever had to fill up forms in a Latin country you will know the kind of questions I mean. For some days past I had been unequal to translating Réaumur into Fahrenheit, but I know that my temperature was round about 103, and by the end of the interview I had some difficulty in standing on my feet. At my back a resigned little knot of patients, carrying bundles done up in coloured handkerchiefs, waited their turn to be questioned.

After the questioning came the bath – a compulsory routine for all newcomers, apparently, just as in prison or the workhouse. My clothes were taken away from me, and after I had sat shivering for some minutes in five inches of warm water I was given a linen nightshirt and a short blue flannel dressing-gown – no slippers, they had none big enough for me, they said – and led out into the open air. This was a night in February and I was suffering from pneumonia. The ward we were going to was 200 yards away and it seemed that to get to it you had to cross the hospital grounds. Someone stumbled in front of me with a lantern. The gravel path was frosty underfoot, and the wind whipped the nightshirt round my bare calves. When we got into the ward I was aware of a strange feeling of familiarity whose origin I did not succeed in pinning down till later in the night. It was a long, rather low, ill-lit room, full of murmuring voices and with three rows of beds surprisingly close together. There was a foul smell, faecal and yet sweetish. As I lay down I saw on a bed nearly opposite me a small, round-shouldered, sandy-haired man sitting half naked while a doctor and a student performed some strange operation on him. First the doctor produced from his black bag a dozen small glasses like wine glasses, then the student burned a match inside each glass to exhaust the air, then the glass was popped on to the man's back or chest and the vacuum drew up a huge yellow blister. Only after some moments did I realize what they were doing to him. It was something called cupping, a treatment which you can read about in old medical text-books but which till then I had vaguely thought of as one of those things they do to horses.

The cold air outside had probably lowered my temperature, and I watched this barbarous remedy with detachment and even a certain amount of amusement. The next moment, however, the doctor and the student came across to my bed, hoisted me upright and without a word began applying the same set of glasses, which had not been sterilized in any way. A few feeble protests that I uttered got no more response than if I had been an animal. I was very much impressed by the impersonal way in which the two men started on me. I had never been in the public ward of a hospital before, and it was my first experience of doctors who handle you without speaking to you or, in a human sense, taking any notice of you. They only put on six glasses in my case, but after doing so they scarified the blisters and applied the glasses again. Each glass now drew about a dessert-spoonful of dark-coloured blood. As I lay down again, humiliated, disgusted and frightened by the thing that had been done to me, I reflected that now at least they would leave me alone. But no, not a bit of it. There was another treatment, coming, the mustard poultice, seemingly a matter of routine like the hot bath. Two slatternly nurses had already got the poultice ready, and they lashed it round my chest as tight as a strait-jacket while some men who were wandering about the ward in shirt and trousers began to collect round my bed with half-sympathetic grins. I learned later that watching a patient have a mustard poultice was a favourite pastime in the ward. These things are normally applied for a quarter of an hour and certainly they are funny enough if you don't happen to be the person inside. For the first five minutes the pain is severe, but you believe you can bear it. During the second five minutes this belief evaporates, but the poultice is buckled at the back and you can't get it off. This is the period the onlookers enjoy most. During the last five minutes, I noted, a sort of numbness supervenes. After the poultice had been removed a waterproof pillow packed with ice was thrust beneath my head and I was left alone. I did not sleep, and to the best of my knowledge this was the only night of my life – I mean the only night spent in bed – in which I have not slept at all, not even a minute.

During my first hour in the Hôpital X I had had a whole series of different and contradictory treatments, but this was misleading, for in general you got very little treatment at all, either good or bad, unless you were ill in some interesting and instructive way. At five in the morning the nurses came round, woke the patients and took their temperatures, but did not wash them. If you were well enough you washed yourself, otherwise you depended on the kindness of some walking patient. It was generally patients, too, who carried the bedbottles and the grim bedpan, nicknamed *la casserole*. At eight breakfast arrived, called army-fashion *la soupe*. It was soup, too, a thin vegetable soup with slimy hunks of bread floating about in it. Later in the day the tall, solemn, black-bearded doctor made his rounds, with an interne and a troop of students following at his heels, but there were about sixty of us in the ward and it was evident that he had other wards to attend to as well. There were many beds past which he walked day after day, sometimes followed by imploring cries. On the other hand if you had some disease with which the students wanted to familiarize themselves you got plenty of attention of a kind. I myself, with an exceptionally fine specimen of a bronchial rattle, sometimes had as many as a dozen students queuing up to listen to my chest. It was a very queer feeling – queer, I mean, because of their intense interest in learning their job, together with a seeming lack of any perception that the patients were human beings. It is strange to relate, but sometimes as some young student stepped forward to take his turn at manipulating you he would be actually tremulous with excitement, like a boy who has at last got his hands on some expensive piece of machinery. And then ear after ear – ears of young men, of girls, of negroes – pressed against your back, relays of fingers solemnly but clumsily tapping, and not from any one of them did you get a word of conversation or a look direct in your face. As a non-paying patient, in the uniform nightshirt, you were primarily *a specimen*, a thing I did not resent but could never quite get used to.

After some days I grew well enough to sit up and study the surrounding patients. The stuffy room, with its narrow beds so close together that you could easily touch your neighbour's hand, had every sort of disease in it except, I suppose, acutely infectious cases. My right-hand neighbour was a little red-haired cobbler with one leg shorter than the other, who used to announce the death of any other patient (this happened a number of times, and my neighbour was always the first to hear of it) by whistling to me, exclaiming 'Numéro 43!' (or whatever it was) and flinging his arms above his head. This man had not much wrong with him, but in most of the other beds within my angle of vision some squalid tragedy or some plain horror was being enacted. In the bed that was foot to foot with mine there lay, until he died (I didn't see him die – they moved him to another bed), a little weazened man who was suffering from I do not know what disease, but something that made his whole body so intensely sensitive that any movement from side to side, sometimes even the weight of the bedclothes, would make him shout out with pain. His worst suffering was when he urinated, which he did with the greatest difficulty. A nurse would bring him the bedbottle and then for a long time stand beside his bed, whistling, as grooms are said to do with horses, until at last with an agonized shriek of *'Je pisse!'* he would get started. In the bed next to him the sandy-haired man whom I had seen being cupped used to cough up blood-streaked mucus at all hours. My left-hand neighbour was a tall, flaccid-looking young man who used periodically to have a tube inserted into his back and astonishing quantities of frothy liquid drawn off from some part of his body. In the bed beyond that a veteran of the war of 1870 was dying, a handsome old man with a white imperial, round whose bed, at all hours when visiting was allowed, four elderly female relatives dressed all in black sat exactly like crows, obviously scheming for some pitiful legacy. In the bed opposite me in the farther row was an old bald-headed man with drooping moustaches and greatly swollen face and body, who was suffering from some disease that made him urinate almost incessantly. A huge glass receptacle stood always beside his bed. One day his wife and daughter came to visit him. At sight of them the old man's bloated face lit up with a smile of surprising sweetness, and as his daughter, a pretty girl of about twenty, approached the bed I saw that his hand was slowly working its way from under the bedclothes. I seemed to see in advance the gesture that was coming – the girl kneeling beside the bed, the old man's hand laid on her head in his dying blessing. But no, he merely handed her the bedbottle, which she promptly took from him and emptied into the receptacle.

About a dozen beds away from me was Numéro 57 – I think that was his number – a cirrhosis-of-the-liver case. Everyone in the ward knew him by sight because he was sometimes the subject of a medical lecture. On two afternoons a week the tall, grave doctor would lecture in the ward to a party of students, and on more than one occasion old Numéro 57 was wheeled in on a sort of trolley into the middle of the ward, where the doctor would roll back his nightshirt, dilate with his fingers a huge flabby protruberance on the man's belly – the diseased liver, I suppose – and explain solemnly that this was a disease attributable to alcoholism, commoner in the wine-drinking countries. As usual he neither spoke to his patient nor gave him a smile, a nod or any kind of recognition. While he talked, very grave and upright, he would hold the wasted body beneath his two hands, sometimes giving it a gentle roll to and fro, in just the attitude of a woman handling a rolling-pin. Not that Numéro 57 minded this kind of thing. Obviously he was an old hospital inmate, a regular exhibit at lectures, his liver long since marked down for a bottle in some pathological museum. Utterly uninterested in what was said about him, he would lie with his colourless eyes gazing at nothing, while the doctor showed him off like a piece of antique china. He was a man of about sixty, astonishingly shrunken. His face, pale as vellum, had shrunken away till it seemed no bigger than a doll's.

One morning my cobbler neighbour woke me up plucking at my pillow before the nurses arrived. 'Numéro 57!' – he flung his arms above his head. There was a light in the ward, enough to see by. I could see old Numéro 57 lying crumpled up on his side, his face sticking out over the side of the bed, and towards me. He had died some time during the night, nobody knew when. When the nurses came they received the news of his death indifferently and went about their work. After a long time, an hour or more, two other nurses marched in abreast like soldiers, with a great clumping of sabots, and knotted the corpse up in the sheets, but it was not removed till some time later. Meanwhile, in the better light, I had had time for a good look at Numéro 57. Indeed I lay on my side to look at him. Curiously enough he was the first dead European I had seen. I had seen dead men before, but always Asiatics and usually people who had died violent deaths. Numéro 57's eyes were still open, his mouth also open, his small face contorted into an expression of agony. What most impressed me, however, was the whiteness of his face. It had been pale before, but now it was little darker than the sheets. As I gazed at the tiny, screwed-up face it struck me that this disgusting piece of refuse, waiting to be carted away and dumped on a slab in the dissecting room, was an example of 'natural' death, one of the things you pray for in the Litany. There you are, then, I thought, that's what is waiting for you, twenty, thirty, forty years hence : that is how the lucky ones die, the ones who live to be old. One wants to live, of course, indeed one only stays alive by virtue of the fear of death, but I think now, as I thought then, that it's better to die violently and not too old. People talk about the horrors of war, but what weapon has man invented that even approaches in cruelty some of the commoner diseases ? 'Natural' death, almost by definition, means something slow, smelly and painful. Even at that, it makes a difference if you can achieve it in your own home and not in a public institution. This poor old wretch who had just flickered out like a candle-end was not even important enough to have anyone watching by his deathbed. He was merely a number, then a 'subject' for the students' scalpels. And the sordid publicity of dying in such a place! In the Hôpital X the beds were very close together and there were no screens. Fancy, for instance, dying like the little man whose bed was for a while foot to foot with mine, the one who cried out when the bedclothes touched him! I dare say '*Je pisse!*' were his last recorded words. Perhaps the dying don't bother about such things – that at least would be the standard answer: nevertheless dying people are often more or less normal in their minds till within a day or so of the end.

In the public wards of a hospital you see horrors that you don't seem to meet with among people who manage to die in their own homes, as though certain diseases only attacked people at the lower income levels. But it is a fact that you would not in any English hospitals see some of the things I saw in the Hôpital X. This business of people just dying like animals, for instance, with nobody standing by, nobody interested, the death not even noticed till the morning – this happened more than once. You certainly would not see that in England, and still less would you see a corpse left exposed to the view of the other patients. I remember that once in a cottage hospital in England a man died while we were at tea, and though there were only six of us in the ward the nurses managed things so adroitly that the man was dead and his body removed without our even hearing about it till tea was over. A thing we perhaps underrate in England is the advantage we enjoy in having large numbers of well-trained and rigidly-disciplined nurses. No doubt English nurses are dumb enough, they may tell fortunes with tea-leaves, wear Union Jack badges and keep photographs of the Queen on their mantelpieces, but at least they don't let you lie unwashed and constipated on an unmade bed, out of sheer laziness. The nurses at the Hôpital X still had a tinge of Mrs Gamp about them, and later, in the military hospitals of Republican Spain, I was to see nurses almost too ignorant to take a temperature. You wouldn't, either, see in England such dirt as existed in the Hôpital X. Later on, when I was well enough to wash myself in the bathroom, I found that there was kept there a huge packing case into which the scraps of food and dirty dressings from the ward were flung, and the wainscotings were infested by crickets. When I had got back my clothes and grown strong on my legs I fled from the Hôpital X, before my time was up and without waiting for a medical discharge. It was not the only hospital I have fled from, but its gloom and bareness, its sickly smell and, above all, something in its mental atmosphere stand out in my memory as exceptional. I had been taken there because it was the hospital belonging to my arrondissement, and I did not learn till after I was in it that it bore a bad reputation. A year or two later the celebrated swindler, Madame Hanaud, who was ill while on remand, was taken to the Hôpital X, and after a few days of it she managed to elude her guards, took a taxi and drove back to the prison, explaining that she was more comfortable there. I have no doubt that the Hôpital X was quite untypical of French hospitals even at that date. But the patients, nearly all of them working men, were surprisingly resigned. Some of them seemed to find the conditions almost comfortable, for at least two were destitute malingerers who found this a good way of getting through the winter. The nurses connived because the malingerers made themselves useful by doing odd jobs. But the attitude of the majority was : of course this is a lousy place, but what else do you expect ? It did not seem strange to them that you should be woken at five and then wait three hours before starting the day on watery soup, or that people should die with no one at their bedside, or even that your

chance of getting medical attention should depend on catch-
ing the doctor's eye as he went past. According to their
traditions that was what hospitals were like. If you are
seriously ill and if you are too poor to be treated in your own
home, then you must go into hospital, and once there you
must put up with harshness and discomfort, just as you would
in the army. But on top of this I was interested to find a
lingering belief in the old stories that have now almost faded
from memory in England – stories, for instance, about doctors cutting you open out of sheer curiosity or thinking it
funny to start operating before you were properly 'under'.
There were dark tales about a little operating-room said to
be situated just beyond the bathroom. Dreadful screams were
said to issue from this room. I saw nothing to confirm these
stories and no doubt they were all nonsense, though I did
see two students kill a sixteen-year-old boy, or nearly kill
him (he appeared to be dying when I left the hospital, but he
may have recovered later) by a mischievous experiment
which they probably could not have tried on a paying
patient. Well within living memory it used to be believed
in London that in some of the big hospitals patients were
killed off to get dissection subjects. I didn't hear this tale
repeated at the Hôpital X, but I should think some of the
men there would have found it credible. For it was a hospital
in which not the methods, perhaps, but something of the
atmosphere of the nineteenth century had managed to survive, and therein lay its peculiar interest.

During the past fifty years or so there has been a great
change in the relationship between doctor and patient. If
you look at almost any literature before the later part of the
nineteenth century, you find that a hospital is popularly
regarded as much the same thing as a prison, and an old-
fashioned, dungeon-like prison at that. A hospital is a place
of filth, torture and death, a sort of antechamber to the

tomb. No one who was not more or less destitute would have thought of going into such a place for treatment. And especially in the early part of the last century, when medical science had grown bolder than before without being any more successful, the whole business of doctoring was looked on with horror and dread by ordinary people. Surgery, in particular, was believed to be no more than a peculiarly gruesome form of sadism, and dissection, possible only with the aid of bodysnatchers, was even confused with necromancy. From the nineteenth century you could collect a large horror-literature connected with doctors and hospitals. Think of poor old George III, in his dotage, shrieking for mercy as he sees his surgeons approaching to 'bleed him till he faints'! Think of the conversations of Bob Sawyer and Benjamin Allen, which no doubt are hardly parodies, or the field hospitals in *La Débâcle* and *War and Peace*, or that shocking description of an amputation in Melville's *White-jacket*! Even the names given to doctors in nineteenth-century English fiction, Slasher, Carver, Sawyer, Fillgrave and so on, and the generic nickname 'sawbones', are about as grim as they are comic. The anti-surgery tradition is perhaps best expressed in Tennyson's poem, *The Children's Hospital,* which is essentially a pre-chloroform document though it seems to have been written as late as 1880. Moreover, the outlook which Tennyson records in this poem had a lot to be said for it. When you consider what an operation without anaesthetics must have been like, what it notoriously *was* like, it is difficult not to suspect the motives of people who would undertake such things. For these bloody horrors which the students so eagerly looked forward to ('A magnificent sight if Slasher does it!') were admittedly more or less useless: the patient who did not die of shock usually died of gangrene, a result which was taken for granted. Even now doctors can be found whose motives are questionable. Anyone who has had much illness, or who has listened to medical students talking, will know what I mean. But anaesthetics were a turning point, and disinfectants were another. Nowhere in the world, probably would you now see the kind of scene described by Axel Munthe in *The Story of San Michele*, when the sinister surgeon in top hat and frock coat, his starched shirtfront spattered with blood and pus, carves up patient after patient with the same knife and flings the severed limbs into a pile beside the table. Moreover, the national health insurance has partly done away with the idea that a working-class patient is a pauper who deserves little consideration. Well into this century it was usual for 'free' patients at the big hospitals to have their teeth extracted with no anaesthetic. They didn't pay, so why should they have an anaesthetic – that was the attitude. That too has changed.

And yet every institution will always bear upon it some lingering memory of its past. A barrack-room is still haunted by the ghost of Kipling, and it is difficult to enter a workhouse without being reminded of *Oliver Twist*. Hospitals began as a kind of casual ward for lepers and the like to die in, and they continued as places where medical students learned their art on the bodies of the poor. You can still catch a faint suggestion of their history in their characteristically gloomy architecture. I would be far from complaining about the treatment I have received in any English hospital, but I do know that it is a sound instinct that warns people to keep out of hospitals if possible, and especially out of the public wards. Whatever the legal position may be, it is unquestionable that you have far less control over your own treatment, far less certainty that frivolous experiments will not be tried on you, when it is a case of 'accept the discipline or get out'. And it is a great thing to die in your own bed, though it is better still to die in your boots. However great the kindness and the efficiency, in every hospital death there will be some cruel, squalid detail, something perhaps too small to be told but leaving terribly painful memories behind, arising out of the haste, the crowding, the impersonality of a place where every day people are dying among strangers.

The dread of hospitals probably still survives among the very poor, and in all of us it has only recently disappeared. It is a dark patch not far beneath the surface of our minds. I have said earlier that when I entered the ward at the Hôpital X I was conscious of a strange feeling of familiarity. What the scene reminded me of, of course, was the reeking, pain-filled hospitals of the nineteenth century, which I had never seen but of which I had a traditional knowledge. And something, perhaps the black-clad doctor with his frowsy black bag, or perhaps only the sickly smell, played the queer trick of unearthing from my memory that poem of Tennyson's, *The Children's Hospital*, which I had not thought of for twenty years. It happened that as a child I had had it read aloud to me by a sick-nurse whose own working life might have stretched back to the time when Tennyson wrote the poem. The horrors and sufferings of the old-style hospitals were a vivid memory to her. We had shuddered over the poem together, and then seemingly I had forgotten it. Even its name would probably have recalled nothing to me. But the first glimpse of the ill-lit murmurous room, with the beds so close together, suddenly roused the train of thought to which it belonged, and in the night that followed I found myself remembering the whole story and atmosphere of the poem, with many of its lines complete.

1946

Rudyard Kipling

It was a pity that Mr Eliot should be so much on the defensive in the long essay with which he prefaces this selection of Kipling's poetry,* but it was not to be avoided, because before one can even speak about Kipling one has to clear away a legend that has been created by two sets of people who have not read his works. Kipling is in the peculiar position of having been a byword for fifty years. During five literary generations every enlightened person has despised him, and at the end of that time nine-tenths of those enlightened persons are forgotten and Kipling is in some sense still there. Mr Eliot never satisfactorily explains this fact, because in answering the shallow and familiar charge that Kipling is a 'Fascist', he falls into the opposite error of defending him where he is not defensible. It is no use pretending that Kipling's view of life, as a whole, can be accepted or even forgiven by any civilized person. It is no use claiming, for instance, that when Kipling describes a British soldier beating a 'nigger' with a cleaning rod in order to get money out of him, he is acting merely as a reporter and does not necessarily approve what he describes. There is not the slightest sign anywhere in Kipling's work that he disapproves of that kind of conduct – on the contrary, there is a definite strain of sadism in him, over and above the brutality which a writer of that type has to have. Kipling *is* a jingo imperialist, he *is* morally insensitive and aesthetically

* *A Choice of Kipling's Verse*, made by T. S. Eliot (Faber & Faber, 8s. 6d.)

disgusting. It is better to start by admitting that, and then to try to find out why it is that he survives while the refined people who have sniggered at him seem to wear so badly.

And yet the 'Fascist' charge has to be answered, because the first clue to any understanding of Kipling, morally or politically, is the fact that he was *not* a Fascist. He was further from being one than the most humane or the most 'progressive' person is able to be nowadays. An interesting instance of the way in which quotations are parroted to and fro without any attempt to look up their context or discover their meaning is the line from 'Recessional', 'Lesser breeds without the Law'. This line is always good for a snigger in pansy-left circles. It is assumed as a matter of course that the 'lesser breeds' are 'natives', and a mental picture is called up of some pukka sahib in a pith helmet kicking a coolie. In its context the sense of the line is almost the exact opposite of this. The phrase 'lesser breeds' refers almost certainly to the Germans, and especially the pan-German writers, who are 'without the Law' in the sense of being lawless, not in the sense of being powerless. The whole poem, conventionally thought of as an orgy of boasting, is a denunciation of power politics, British as well as German. Two stanzas are worth quoting (I am quoting this as politics, not as poetry):

> If, drunk with sight of power, we loose
> Wild tongues that have not Thee in awe,
> Such boastings as the Gentiles use,
> Or lesser breeds without the Law –
> Lord God of hosts, be with us yet,
> Lest we forget – lest we forget!

> For heathen heart that puts her trust
> In reeking tube and iron shard,
> All valiant dust that builds on dust,

And guarding, calls not Thee to guard,
For frantic boast and foolish word –
Thy mercy on Thy People, Lord!

Much of Kipling's phraseology is taken from the Bible, and no doubt in the second stanza he had in mind the text from Psalm cxxvii: 'Except the lord build the house, they labour in vain that build it; except the Lord keep the city, the watchman waketh but in vain.' It is not a text that makes much impression on the post-Hitler mind. No one, in our time, believes in any sanction greater than military power; no one believes that it is possible to overcome force except by greater force. There is no 'Law', there is only power. I am not saying that that is a true belief, merely that it is the belief which all modern men do actually hold. Those who pretend otherwise are either intellectual cowards, or power-worshippers under a thin disguise, or have simply not caught up with the age they are living in. Kipling's outlook is prefascist. He still believes that pride comes before a fall and that the gods punish *hubris*. He does not foresee the tank, the bombing plane, the radio and the secret police, or their psychological results.

But in saying this, does not one unsay what I said above about Kipling's jingoism and brutality? No, one is merely saying that the nineteenth-century imperialist outlook and the modern gangster outlook are two different things. Kipling belongs very definitely to the period 1885–1902. The Great War and its aftermath embittered him, but he shows little sign of having learned anything from any event later than the Boer War. He was the prophet of British Imperialism in its expansionist phase (even more than his poems, his solitary novel, *The Light that Failed*, gives you the atmosphere of that time) and also the unofficial historian of the British Army, the old mercenary army which began to change its shape in 1914. All his confidence, his bouncing vulgar vitality, sprang out of limitations which no Fascist or near-Fascist shares.

Kipling spent the later part of his life in sulking, and no doubt it was political disappointment rather than literary vanity that account for this. Somehow history had not gone according to plan. After the greatest victory she had ever known, Britain was a lesser world power than before, and Kipling was quite acute enough to see this. The virtue had gone out of the classes he idealized, the young were hedonistic or disaffected, the desire to paint the map red had evaporated. He could not understand what was happening, because he had never had any grasp of the economic forces underlying imperial expansion. It is notable that Kipling does not seem to realize, any more than the average soldier or colonial administrator, that an empire is primarily a money-making concern. Imperialism as he sees it is a sort of forcible evangelizing. You turn a Gatling gun on a mob of unarmed 'natives', and then you establish 'the Law', which includes roads, railways and a court-house. He could not foresee, therefore, that the same motives which brought the Empire into existence would end by destroying it. It was the same motive, for example, that caused the Malayan jungles to be cleared for rubber estates, and which now causes those estates to be handed over intact to the Japanese. The modern totalitarians know what they are doing, and the nineteenth-century English did not know what they were doing. Both attitudes have their advantages, but Kipling was never able to move forward from one into the other. His outlook, allowing for the fact that after all he was an artist, was that of the salaried bureaucrat who despises the 'box-wallah' and often lives a lifetime without realizing that the 'box-wallah' calls the tune.

But because he identifies himself with the official class, he does possess one thing which 'enlightened' people seldom or never possess, and that is a sense of responsibility. The middle-class Left hate him for this quite as much as for his cruelty and vulgarity. All left-wing parties in the highly industrialized countries are at bottom a sham, because they make it their business to fight against something which they do not really wish to destroy. They have internationalist aims, and at the same time they struggle to keep up a standard of life with which those aims are incompatible. We all live by robbing Asiatic coolies, and those of us who are 'enlightened' all maintain that those coolies ought to be set free; but our standard of living, and hence our 'enlightenment', demands that the robbery shall continue. A humanitarian is always a hypocrite, and Kipling's understanding of this is perhaps the central secret of his power to create telling phrases. It would be difficult to hit off the one-eyed pacifism of the English in fewer words than in the phrase, 'making mock of uniforms that guard you while you sleep'. It is true that Kipling does not understand the economic aspect of the relationship between the highbrow and the blimp. He does not see that the map is painted red chiefly in order that the coolie may be exploited. Instead of the coolie he sees the Indian Civil Servant; but even on that plane his grasp of function, of who protects whom, is very sound. He sees clearly that men can only be highly civilized while other men, inevitably less civilized, are there to guard and feed them.

How far does Kipling really identify himself with the administrators, soldiers and engineers whose praises he sings? Not so completely as is sometimes assumed. He had travelled very widely while he was still a young man, he had grown up with a brilliant mind in mainly philistine surroundings, and some streak in him that may have been partly neurotic led him to prefer the active man to the sensitive man. The nineteenth-century Anglo-Indians, to name the least sympathetic of his idols, were at any rate people who did things. It may be that all that they did was evil, but they changed the face of the earth (it is instructive to look at a map of Asia and compare the railway system of India with that of the surrounding countries), whereas they could have achieved nothing, could not have maintained themselves in power for a single week, if the normal Anglo-Indian outlook had been that of, say, E. M. Forster. Tawdry and shallow though it is, Kipling's is the only literary picture that we possess of nineteenth-century Anglo-India, and he could only make it because he was just coarse enough to be able to exist and keep his mouth shut in clubs and regimental messes. But he did not greatly resemble the people he admired. I know from several private sources that many of the Anglo-Indians who were Kipling's contemporaries did not like or approve of him. They said, no doubt truly, that he knew nothing about India, and on the other hand, he was from their point of view too much of a highbrow. While in India he tended to mix with 'the wrong' people, and because of his dark complexion he was wrongly suspected of having a streak of Asiatic blood. Much in his development is traceable to his having been born in India and having left school early. With a slightly different background he might have been a good novelist or a superlative writer of music-hall songs. But how true is it that he was a vulgar flag-waver, a sort of publicity agent for Cecil Rhodes? It is true, but it is not true that he was a yes-man or a time-server. After his early days, if then, he never courted public opinion. Mr Eliot says that what is held against him is that he expressed unpopular views in a popular style. This narrows the issue by assuming that 'unpopular' means unpopular with the intelligentsia, but it is a fact that Kipling's 'message' was one that the big public did not want, and, indeed, has never accepted. The mass of the people, in the nineties as now, were anti-militarist, bored by the Empire, and only unconsciously patriotic. Kipling's official admirers are and were the 'service' middle class, the people who read *Black-wood's*. In the stupid early years of this century, the blimps, having at last discovered someone who could be called a poet and who was on their side, set Kipling on a pedestal, and some of his more sententious poems, such as 'If', were given almost biblical status. But it is doubtful whether the blimps have ever read him with attention, any more than they have read the Bible. Much of what he says they could not possibly approve. Few people who have criticized England from the inside have said bitterer things about her than this gutter patriot. As a rule it is the British working class that he is attacking, but not always. That phrase about 'the flannelled fools at the wicket and the muddied oafs at the goal' sticks like an arrow to this day, and it is aimed at the Eton and Harrow match as well as the Cup-Tie Final. Some of the verses he wrote about the Boer War have a curiously modern ring, so far as their subject-matter goes. 'Stellenbosch', which must have been written about 1902, sums up what every intelligent infantry officer was saying in 1918, or is saying now, for that matter.

Kipling's romantic ideas about England and the Empire might not have mattered if he could have held them without having the class-prejudices which at that time went with them. If one examines his best and most representative work, his soldier poems, especially *Barrack-Room Ballads*, one notices that what more than anything else spoils them is an underlying air of patronage. Kipling idealizes the army officer, especially the junior officer, and that to an idiotic extent, but the private soldier, though lovable and romantic, has to be a comic. He is always made to speak in a sort of stylized Cockney, not very broad but with all the aitches and final 'g's' carefully omitted. Very often the result is as

embarrassing as the humorous recitation at a church social.
And this accounts for the curious fact that one can often
improve Kipling's poems, make them less facetious and less
blatant, by simply going through them and transplanting
them from Cockney into standard speech. This is especially
true of his refrains, which often have a truly lyrical quality.
Two examples will do (one is about a funeral and the other
about a wedding) :

> So it's knock out your pipes and follow me !
> And it's finish up your swipes and follow me !
> Oh, hark to the big drum calling,
> Follow me – follow me home !

and again :

> Cheer for the Sergeant's wedding –
> Give them one cheer more !
> Grey gun-horses in the lando,
> And a rogue is married to a whore !

Here I have restored the aitches, etc. Kipling ought to have
known better. He ought to have seen that the two closing
lines of the first of these stanzas are very beautiful lines, and
that ought to have overriden his impulse to make fun of a
working-man's accent. In the ancient ballads the lord and
the peasant speak the same language. This is impossible to
Kipling, who is looking down a distorting class-perspective,
and by a piece of poetic justice one of his best lines is spoiled
– for 'follow me 'ome' is much uglier than 'follow me
home'. But even where it makes no difference musically
the facetiousness of his stage Cockney dialect is irritating.
However, he is more often quoted aloud than read on the
printed page, and most people instinctively make the necessary alterations when they quote him.

Can one imagine any private soldier, in the nineties or

now, reading *Barrack-Room Ballads* and feeling that here was a writer who spoke for him? It is very hard to do so. Any soldier capable of reading a book of verse would notice at once that Kipling is almost unconscious of the class war that goes on in an army as much as elsewhere. It is not only that he thinks the soldier comic, but that he thinks him patriotic, feudal, a ready admirer of his officers and proud to be a soldier of the Queen. Of course that is partly true, or battles could not be fought, but 'What have I done for thee, England, my England?' is essentially a middle-class query. Almost any working man would follow it up immediately with 'What has England done for me?' In so far as Kipling grasps this, he simply sets it down to 'the intense selfishness of the lower classes' (his own phrase). When he is writing not of British but of 'loyal' Indians he carries the 'Salaam, sahib' motif to sometimes disgusting lengths. Yet it remains true that he has far more interest in the common soldier, far more anxiety that he shall get a fair deal, than most of the 'liberals' of his day or our own. He sees that the soldier is neglected, meanly underpaid and hypocritically despised by the people whose incomes he safeguards. 'I came to realize', he says in his posthumous memoirs, 'the bare horrors of the private's life, and the unnecessary torments he endured.' He is accused of glorifying war, and perhaps he does so, but not in the usual manner, by pretending that war is a sort of football match. Like most people capable of writing battle poetry, Kipling had never been in battle, but his vision of war is realistic. He knows that bullets hurt, that under fire everyone is terrified, that the ordinary soldier never knows what the war is about or what is happening except in his own corner of the battlefield, and that British troops, like other troops, frequently run away:

> I 'eard the knives be'ind me, but I dursn't face my man,
> Nor I don't know where I went to, 'cause I didn't stop to see,
> Till I 'eard a beggar squealin' out for quarter as 'e ran,
> An' I thought I knew the voice an' – it was me!

Modernize the style of this, and it might have come out of one of the debunking war books of the nineteen-twenties. Or again:

> An' now the hugly bullets come peckin' through the dust,
> An' no one wants to face 'em, but every beggar must;
> So, like a man in irons, which isn't glad to go,
> They moves 'em off by companies uncommon stiff an' slow.

Compare this with:

> Forward the Light Brigade!
> Was there a man dismayed?
> No! though the soldier knew
> Someone had blundered.

If anything, Kipling overdoes the horrors, for the wars of his youth were hardly wars at all by our standards. Perhaps that is due to the neurotic strain in him, the hunger for cruelty. But at least he knows that men ordered to attack impossible objectives *are* dismayed, and also that fourpence a day is not a generous pension.

How complete or truthful a picture has Kipling left us of the long-service, mercenary army of the late nineteenth century? One must say of this, as of what Kipling wrote about nineteenth-century Anglo-India, that it is not only the best but almost the only literary picture we have. He has put on record an immense amount of stuff that one could otherwise only gather from verbal tradition or from unreadable regimental histories. Perhaps his picture of army life seems fuller and more accurate than it is because any middle-class English person is likely to know enough to fill up the gaps. At any rate, reading the essay on Kipling that Mr Edmund

Wilson has just published or is just about to publish,* I was struck by the number of things that are boringly familiar to us and seem to be barely intelligible to an American. But from the body of Kipling's early work there does seem to emerge a vivid and not seriously misleading picture of the old pre-machine-gun army – the sweltering barracks in Gibraltar or Lucknow, the red coats, the pipeclayed belts and the pillbox hats, the beer, the fights, the floggings, hangings and crucifixions, the bugle-calls, the smell of oats and horse-piss, the bellowing sergeants with foot-long moustaches, the bloody skirmishes, invariably mismanaged, the crowded troopships, the cholera-stricken camps, the 'native' concubines, the ultimate death in the workhouse. It is a crude, vulgar picture, in which a patriotic music-hall turn seems to have got mixed up with one of Zola's gorier passages, but from it future generations will be able to gather some idea of what a long-term volunteer army was like. On about the same level they will be able to learn something of British India in the days when motor-cars and refrigerators were unheard of. It is an error to imagine that we might have had better books on these subjects if, for example, George Moore, or Gissing, or Thomas Hardy, had had Kipling's opportunities. That is the kind of accident that cannot happen. It was not possible that nineteenth-century England should produce a book like *War and Peace*, or like Tolstoy's minor stories of army life, such as *Sebastopol* or *The Cossacks*, not because the talent was necessarily lacking but because no one with sufficient sensitiveness to write such books would ever have made the appropriate contacts. Tolstoy lived in a great military empire in which it seemed natural for almost any young man of family to spend a few years in the army, whereas the British Empire was and still is

* 1945. Published in a volume of Collected Essays, *The Wound and the Bow* (Secker & Warburg).

demilitarized to a degree which continental observers find almost incredible. Civilized men do not readily move away from the centres of civilization, and in most languages there is a great dearth of what one might call colonial literature. It took a very improbable combination of circumstances to produce Kipling's gaudy tableau, in which Private Ortheris and Mrs Hauksbee pose against a background of palm trees to the sound of temple bells, and one necessary circumstance was that Kipling himself was only half civilized.

Kipling is the only English writer of our time who has added phrases to the language. The phrases and neologisms which we take over and use without remembering their origin do not always come from writers we admire. It is strange, for instance, to hear the Nazi broadcasters referring to the Russian soldiers as 'robots', thus unconsciously borrowing a word from a Czech democrat whom they would have killed if they could have laid hands on him. Here are half a dozen phrases coined by Kipling which one sees quoted in leaderettes in the gutter press or overhears in saloon bars from people who have barely heard his name. It will be seen that they all have a certain characteristic in common :

> East is East, and West is West.
> The white man's burden.
> What do they know of England who only England know ?
> The female of the species is more deadly than the male.
> Somewhere East of Suez.
> Paying the Dane-geld.

There are various others, including some that have outlived their context by many years. The phrase 'killing Kruger with your mouth', for instance, was current till very recently. It is also possible that it was Kipling who first let loose the use of the word 'Huns' for Germans; at any rate he began using it as soon as the guns opened fire in 1914.

But what the phrases I have listed above have in common is that they are all of them phrases which one utters semi-derisively (as it might be 'For I'm to be Queen o' the May, mother, I'm to be Queen o' the May), but which one is bound to make use of sooner or later. Nothing could exceed the contempt of the *New Statesman*, for instance, for Kipling, but how many times during the Munich period did the *New Statesman* find itself quoting that phrase about paying the Dane-geld ? * The fact is that Kipling, apart from his snack-bar wisdom and his gift for packing much cheap picturesqueness into a few words ('palm and pine' – 'east of Suez' – 'the road to Mandalay'), is generally talking about things that are of urgent interest. It does not matter, from this point of view, that thinking and decent people generally find themselves on the other side of the fence from him. 'White man's burden' instantly conjures up a real problem, even if one feels that it ought to be altered to 'black man's burden'. One may disagree to the middle of one's bones with the political attitude implied in 'The Islanders', but one cannot say that it is a frivolous attitude. Kipling deals in thoughts which are both vulgar and permanent. This raises the question of his special status as a poet, or verse-writer.

Mr Eliot describes Kipling's metrical work as 'verse' and not 'poetry', but adds that it is '*great* verse', and further qualifies this by saying that a writer can only be described

* 1945. On the first page of his recent book, *Adam and Eve*, Mr Middleton Murry quotes the well-known lines:

> 'There are nine and sixty ways
>   Of constructing tribal lays,
>   And every single one of them is right.'

He attributes these lines to Thackeray. This is probably what is known as a 'Freudian error'. A civilized person would prefer not to quote Kipling – i.e. would prefer not to feel that it was Kipling who had expressed his thought for him.

as a 'great verse-writer' if there is some of his work 'of which we cannot say whether it is verse or poetry'. Apparently Kipling was a versifier who occasionally wrote poems, in which case it was a pity that Mr Eliot did not specify these poems by name. The trouble is that whenever an aesthetic judgement on Kipling's work seems to be called for, Mr Eliot is too much on the defensive to be able to speak plainly. What he does not say, and what I think one ought to start by saying in any discussion of Kipling, is that most of Kipling's verse is so horribly vulgar that it gives one the same sensation as one gets from watching a third-rate music-hall performer recite 'The Pigtail of Wu Fang Fu' with the purple limelight on his face, *and yet* there is much of it that is capable of giving pleasure to people who know what poetry means. At his worst, and also his most vital, in poems like 'Gunga Din' or 'Danny Deever', Kipling is almost a shameful pleasure, like the taste for cheap sweets that some people secretly carry into middle life. But even with his best passages one has the same sense of being seduced by something spurious, and yet unquestionably seduced. Unless one is merely a snob and a liar it is impossible to say that no one who cares for poetry could get any pleasure out of such lines as:

For the wind is in the palm trees, and the temple bells they say,
'Come you back, you British soldier, come you back to
Mandalay!'

and yet those lines are not poetry in the same sense as 'Felix Randal' or 'When icicles hang by the wall' are poetry. One can, perhaps, place Kipling more satisfactorily than by juggling with the words 'verse' and 'poetry', if one describes him simply as a good bad poet. He is as a poet what Harriet Beecher Stowe was as a novelist. And the mere existence of work of this kind, which is perceived by generation after generation to be vulgar and yet goes on being read, tells one something about the age we live in.

There is a great deal of good bad poetry in English, all of it, I should say, subsequent to 1790. Examples of good bad poems – I am deliberately choosing diverse ones – are 'The Bridge of Sighs', 'When all the world is young, lad', 'The Charge of the Light Brigade', Bret Harte's 'Dickens in Camp', 'The Burial of Sir John Moore', 'Jenny Kissed Me', 'Keith of Ravelston', 'Casabianca'. All of these reek of sentimentality, and yet – not these particular poems, perhaps, but poems of this kind, are capable of giving true pleasure to people who can see clearly what is wrong with them. One could fill a fair-sized anthology with good bad poems, if it were not for the significant fact that good bad poetry is usually too well known to be worth reprinting. It is no use pretending that in an age like our own, 'good' poetry can have any genuine popularity. It is, and must be, the cult of a very few people, the least tolerated of the arts. Perhaps that statement needs a certain amount of qualification. True poetry can sometimes be acceptable to the mass of the people when it disguises itself as something else. One can see an example of this in the folk-poetry that England still possesses, certain nursery rhymes and mnemonic rhymes, for instance, and the songs that soldiers make up, including the words that go to some of the bugle-calls. But in general ours is a civilization in which the very word 'poetry' evokes a hostile snigger or, at best, the sort of frozen disgust that most people feel when they hear the word 'God'. If you are good at playing the concertina you could probably go into the nearest public bar and get yourself an appreciative audience within five minutes. But what would be the attitude of that same audience if you suggested reading them Shakespeare's sonnets, for instance? Good bad poetry, however, can get across to the most unpromising audiences if the right atmosphere has been worked up beforehand. Some months back Churchill produced a great effect by quoting Clough's 'Endeavour' in one of his broadcast speeches. I listened to this speech among people who could certainly not be accused of caring for poetry, and I am convinced that the lapse into verse impressed them and did not embarrass them. But not even Churchill could have got away with it if he had quoted anything much better than this.

In so far as a writer of verse can be popular, Kipling has been and probably still is popular. In his own lifetime some of his poems travelled far beyond the bounds of the reading public, beyond the world of school prize-days, Boy Scout singsongs, limp-leather editions, pokerwork and calendars, and out into the yet vaster world of the music halls. Nevertheless, Mr Eliot thinks it worth while to edit him, thus confessing to a taste which others share but are not always honest enough to mention. The fact that such a thing as good bad poetry can exist is a sign of the emotional overlap between the intellectual and the ordinary man. The intellectual *is* different from the ordinary man, but only in certain sections of his personality, and even then not all the time. But what is the peculiarity of a good bad poem? A good bad poem is a graceful monument to the obvious. It records in memorable form – for verse is a mnemonic device, among other things – some emotion which very nearly every human being can share. The merit of a poem like 'When all the world is young, lad' is that, however sentimental it may be, its sentiment is 'true' sentiment in the sense that you are bound to find yourself thinking the thought it expresses sooner or later; and then, if you happen to know the poem, it will come back into your mind and seem better than it did before. Such poems are a kind of rhyming proverb, and it is a fact that definitely popular poetry is usually gnomic or sententious. One example from Kipling will do:

> White hands cling to the bridle rein,
> Slipping the spur from the booted heel;
> Tenderest voices cry 'Turn again!'
> Red lips tarnish the scabbarded steel:
> Down to Gehenna or up to the Throne,
> He travels the fastest who travels alone.

There is a vulgar thought vigorously expressed. It may not be true, but at any rate it is a thought that everyone thinks. Sooner or later you will have occasion to feel that he travels the fastest who travels alone, and there the thought is, ready made and, as it were, waiting for you. So the chances are that, having once heard this line, you will remember it.

One reason for Kipling's power as a good bad poet I have already suggested – his sense of responsibility, which made it possible for him to have a world-view, even though it happened to be a false one. Although he had no direct connexion with any political party, Kipling was a Conservative, a thing that does not exist nowadays. Those who now call themselves Conservatives are either Liberals, Fascists or the accomplices of Fascists. He identified himself with the ruling power and not with the opposition. In a gifted writer this seems to us strange and even disgusting, but it did have the advantage of giving Kipling a certain grip on reality. The ruling power is always faced with the question, 'In such and such circumstances, what would you *do*?', whereas the opposition is not obliged to take responsibility or make any real decisions. Where it is a permanent and pensioned opposition, as in England, the quality of its thought deteriorates accordingly. Moreover, anyone who starts out with a pessimistic, reactionary view of life tends to be justified by events, for Utopia never arrives and 'the gods of the copybook headings', as Kipling himself put it, always return. Kipling sold out to the British governing class, not financially but emotionally. This warped his political judgement, for the British ruling class were not what he imagined, and it led him into abysses of folly and snobbery, but he gained a corresponding advantage from having at least tried to imagine what action and responsibility are like. It is a great thing in his favour that he is not witty, not 'daring', has no wish to *épater les bourgeois*. He dealt largely in platitudes, and since we live in a world of platitudes, much of what he said sticks. Even his worst follies seem less shallow and less irritating than the 'enlightened' utterances of the same period, such as Wilde's epigrams or the collection of cracker-mottoes at the end of *Man and Superman*.

.1942

Raffles and Miss Blandish

Nearly half a century after his first appearance, Raffles, 'the amateur cracksman', is still one of the best-known characters in English fiction. Very few people would need telling that he played cricket for England, had bachelor chambers in the Albany and burgled the Mayfair houses which he also entered as a guest. Just for that reason he and his exploits make a suitable background against which to examine a more modern crime story such as *No Orchids for Miss Blandish*. Any such choice is necessarily arbitrary – I might equally well have chosen *Arsène Lupin* for instance – but at any rate *No Orchids* and the Raffles books* have the common quality of being crime stories which play the limelight on the criminal rather than the policeman. For sociological purposes they can be compared. *No Orchids* is the 1939 version of glamorized crime, *Raffles* the 1900 version. What I am concerned with here is the immense difference in moral atmosphere between the two books, and the change in the popular attitude that this probably implies.

At this date, the charm of *Raffles* is partly in the period atmosphere and partly in the technical excellence of the stories. Hornung was a very conscientious and on his level a very able writer. Anyone who cares for sheer efficiency

* *Raffles, A Thief in the Night* and *Mr Justice Raffles*, by E. W. Hornung. The third of these is definitely a failure, and only the first has the true Raffles atmosphere. Hornung wrote a number of crime stories, usually with a tendency to take the side of the criminal. A successful book in rather the same vein as *Raffles* is *Stingaree*.

must admire his work. However, the truly dramatic thing about Raffles, the thing that makes him a sort of byword even to this day (only a few weeks ago, in a burglary case, a magistrate referred to the prisoner as 'a Raffles in real life'), is the fact that he is *a gentleman*. Raffles is presented to us – and this is rubbed home in countless scraps of dialogue and casual remarks – not as an honest man who has gone astray, but as a public-school man who has gone astray. His remorse, when he feels any, is almost purely social; he has disgraced 'the old school', he has lost his right to enter 'decent society', he has forfeited his amateur status and become a cad. Neither Raffles nor Bunny appears to feel at all strongly that stealing is wrong in itself, though Raffles does once justify himself by the casual remark that 'the distribution of property is all wrong anyway'. They think of themselves not as sinners but as renegades, or simply as outcasts. And the moral code of most of us is still so close to Raffles' own that we do feel his situation to be an especially ironical one. A West End club man who is really a burglar! That is almost a story in itself, is it not? But how if it were a plumber or a greengrocer who was really a burglar? Would there be anything inherently dramatic in that? No – although the theme of the 'double life', of respectability covering crime, is still there. Even Charles Peace in his clergyman's dog-collar, seems somewhat less of a hypocrite than Raffles in his Zingari blazer.

Raffles, of course, is good at all games, but it is peculiarly fitting that his chosen game should be cricket. This allows not only of endless analogies between his cunning as a slow bowler and his cunning as a burglar, but also helps to define the exact nature of his crime. Cricket is not in reality a very popular game in England – it is nowhere so popular as football, for instance – but it gives expression to a well-marked trait in the English character, the tendency to value 'form' or 'style' more highly than success. In the eyes of any true cricket-lover it is possible for an innings of ten runs to be 'better' (*i.e.* more elegant) than an innings of a hundred runs: cricket is also one of the very few games in which the amateur can excel the professional. It is a game full of forlorn hopes and sudden dramatic changes of fortune, and its rules are so defined that their interpretation is partly an ethical business. When Larwood, for instance, practised body-line bowling in Australia he was not actually breaking any rule: he was merely doing something that was 'not cricket'. Since cricket takes up a lot of time and is rather an expensive game to play, it is predominantly an upper-class game, but for the whole nation it is bound up with such concepts as 'good form', 'playing the game', etc., and it has declined in popularity just as the tradition of 'don't hit a man when he's down' has declined. It is not a twentieth-century game, and nearly all modern-minded people dislike it. The Nazis, for instance, were at pains to discourage cricket, which had gained a certain footing in Germany before and after the last war. In making Raffles a cricketer as well as a burglar, Hornung was not merely providing him with a plausible disguise; he was also drawing the sharpest moral contrast that he was able to imagine.

Raffles, no less than *Great Expectations* or *Le Rouge et le Noir*, is a story of snobbery, and it gains a great deal from the precariousness of Raffles's social position. A cruder writer would have made the 'gentleman burglar' a member of the peerage, or at least a baronet. Raffles, however, is of upper-middle-class origin and is only accepted by the aristocracy because of his personal charm. 'We were in Society but not of it', he says to Bunny towards the end of the book;

and 'I was asked about for my cricket'. Both he and Bunny accept the values of 'Society' unquestioningly, and would settle down in it for good if only they could get away with a big enough haul. The ruin that constantly threatens them is all the blacker because they only doubtfully 'belong'. A duke who has served a prison sentence is still a duke, whereas a mere man about town, if once disgraced, ceases to be 'about town' for evermore. The closing chapters of the book, when Raffles has been exposed and is living under an assumed name, have a twilight of the gods feeling, a mental atmosphere rather similar to that of Kipling's poem, 'Gentleman Rankers':

> Yes, a trooper of the forces –
> Who has run his own six horses! etc.

Raffles now belongs irrevocably to the 'cohorts of the damned'. He can still commit successful burglaries, but there is no way back into Paradise, which means Piccadilly and the M.C.C. According to the public-school code there is only one means of rehabilitation : death in battle. Raffles dies fighting against the Boers (a practised reader would foresee this from the start), and in the eyes of both Bunny and his creator this cancels his crimes.

Both Raffles and Bunny, of course, are devoid of religious belief, and they have no real ethical code, merely certain rules of behaviour which they observe semi-instinctively. But it is just here that the deep moral difference between *Raffles* and *No Orchids* becomes apparent. Raffles and Bunny, after all, are gentlemen, and such standards as they do have are not to be violated. Certain things are 'not done', and the idea of doing them hardly arises. Raffles will not, for example, abuse hospitality. He will commit a burglary in a house where he is staying as a guest, but the victim must be a fellow-guest and not the host. He will not commit murder,* and he avoids violence wherever possible and prefers to carry out his robberies unarmed. He regards friendship as sacred, and is chivalrous though not moral in his relations with women. He will take extra risks in the name of 'sportsmanship', and sometimes even for aesthetic reasons. And above all, he is intensively patriotic. He celebrates the Diamond Jubilee ('For sixty years, Bunny, we've been ruled over by absolutely the finest sovereign the world has ever seen') by dispatching to the Queen, through the post, an antique gold cup which he has stolen from the British Museum. He steals, from partly political motives, a pearl which the German Emperor is sending to one of the enemies of Britain, and when the Boer War begins to go badly his one thought is to find his way into the fighting line. At the front he unmasks a spy at the cost of revealing his own identity, and then dies gloriously by a Boer bullet. In this combination of crime and patriotism he resembles his near-contemporary Arsène Lupin, who also scores off the German Emperor and wipes out his very dirty past by enlisting in the Foreign Legion.

It is important to note that by modern standards Raffles's crimes are very petty ones. Four hundred pounds' worth of jewellery seems to him an excellent haul. And though the stories are convincing in their physical detail, they contain very little sensationalism – very few corpses, hardly any blood, no sex crimes, no sadism, no perversions of any kind. It seems to be the case that the crime story, at any rate on its higher levels, has greatly increased in blood-thirstiness during

* 1945. Actually Raffles does kill one man and is more or less consciously responsible for the death of two others. But all three of them are foreigners and have behaved in a very reprehensible manner. He also, on one occasion, contemplates murdering a blackmailer. It is however, a fairly well-established convention in crime stories that murdering a blackmailer 'doesn't count'.

the past twenty years. Some of the early detective stories do not even contain a murder. The Sherlock Holmes stories, for instance, are not all murders, and some of them do not even deal with an indictable crime. So also with the John Thorndyke stories, while of the Max Carrados stories only a minority are murders. Since 1918, however, a detective story not containing a murder has been a great rarity, and the most disgusting details of dismemberment and exhumation are commonly exploited. Some of the Peter Wimsey stories, for instance, display an extremely morbid interest in corpses. The Raffles stories, written from the angle of the criminal, are much less anti-social than many modern stories written from the angle of the detective. The main impression that they leave behind is of boyishness. They belong to a time when people had standards, though they happened to be foolish standards. Their key-phrase is 'not done'. The line that they draw between good and evil is as senseless as a Polynesian taboo, but at least, like the taboo, it has the advantage that everyone accepts it.

So much for *Raffles*. Now for a header into the cesspool. *No Orchids for Miss Blandish*, by James Hadley Chase, was published in 1939, but seems to have enjoyed its greatest popularity in 1940, during the Battle of Britain and the blitz. In its main outlines its story is this:

Miss Blandish, the daughter of a millionaire, is kidnapped by some gangsters who are almost immediately surprised and killed off by a larger and better organized gang. They hold her to ransom and extract half a million dollars from her father. Their original plan had been to kill her as soon as the ransom-money was received, but a chance keeps her alive. One of the gang is a young man named Slim, whose sole pleasure in life consists in driving knives into other people's bellies. In childhood he has graduated by cutting up living animals with a pair of rusty scissors. Slim is sexually impotent, but takes a kind of fancy to Miss Bland-ish. Slim's mother, who is the real brains of the gang, sees in this the chance of curing Slim's impotence, and decides to keep Miss Blandish in custody till Slim shall have succeeded in raping her. After many efforts and much persuasion, including the flogging of Miss Blandish with a length of rubber hosepipe, the rape is achieved. Meanwhile Miss Blandish's father has hired a private detective, and by means of bribery and torture the detective and the police manage to round up and exterminate the whole gang. Slim escapes with Miss Blandish and is killed after a final rape, and the detective prepares to restore Miss Blandish to her family. By this time, however, she has developed such a taste for Slim's caresses* that she feels unable to live without him, and she jumps out of the window of a sky-scraper.

Several other points need noticing before one can grasp the full implications of this book. To begin with, its central story bears a very marked resemblance to William Faulkner's novel, *Sanctuary*. Secondly, it is not, as one might expect, the product of an illiterate hack, but a brilliant piece of writing, with hardly a wasted word or a jarring note anywhere. Thirdly, the whole book, *récit* as well as dialogue, is written in the American language; the author, an Englishman who has (I believe) never been in the United States, seems to have made a complete mental transference to the American underworld. Fourthly, the book sold, according to its publishers, no less than half a million copies.

I have already outlined the plot, but the subject-matter is much more sordid and brutal than this suggests. The book contains eight full-dress murders, an unassessable number of

---

*1945. Another reading of the final episode is possible. It may mean merely that Miss Blandish is pregnant. But the interpretation I have given above seems more in keeping with the general brutality of the book.

casual killings and woundings, an exhumation (with a careful reminder of the stench), the flogging of Miss Blandish, the torture of another woman with red-hot cigarette-ends, a strip-tease act, a third-degree scene of unheard-of cruelty and much else of the same kind. It assumes great sexual sophistication in its readers (there is a scene, for instance, in which a gangster, presumably of masochistic tendency, has an orgasm in the moment of being knifed), and it takes for granted the most complete corruption and self-seeking as the norm of human behaviour. The detective, for instance, is almost as great a rogue as the gangsters, and actuated by nearly the same motives. Like them, he is in pursuit of 'five hundred grand'. It is necessary to the machinery of the story that Mr Blandish should be anxious to get his daughter back, but apart from this, such things as affection, friendship, good nature or even ordinary politeness simply do not enter. Nor, to any great extent does normal sexuality. Ultimately only one motive is at work throughout the whole story : the pursuit of power.

It should be noticed that the book is not in the ordinary sense pornography. Unlike most books that deal in sexual sadism, it lays the emphasis on the cruelty and not on the pleasure. Slim, the ravisher of Miss Blandish, has 'wet slobbering lips' : this is disgusting, and it is meant to be disgusting. But the scenes describing cruelty to women are comparatively perfunctory. The real high-spots of the book are cruelties committed by men upon other men : above all, the third-degreeing of the gangster, Eddie Schultz, who is lashed into a chair and flogged on the windpipe with truncheons, his arms broken by fresh blows as he breaks loose. In another of Mr Chase's books, *He Won't Need It Now*, the hero, who is intended to be a sympathetic and perhaps even noble character, is described as stamping on somebody's face, and then, having crushed the man's mouth in, grinding his heel round and round in it. Even when physical incidents of this kind are not occurring, the mental atmosphere of these books is always the same. Their whole theme is the struggle for power and the triumph of the strong over the weak. The big gangsters wipe out the little ones as mercilessly as a pike gobbling up the little fish in a pond; the police kill off the criminals as cruelly as the angler kills the pike. If ultimately one sides with the police against the gangsters, it is merely because they are better organized and more powerful, because, in fact, the law is a bigger racket than crime. Might is right: *vae victis*.

As I have mentioned already, *No Orchids* enjoyed its greatest vogue in 1940, though it was successfully running as a play till some time later. It was, in fact, one of the things that helped to console people for the boredom of being bombed. Early in the war the *New Yorker* had a picture of a little man approaching a news-stall littered with paper with such headlines as 'Great Tank Battles in Northern France', 'Big Naval Battle in the North Sea', 'Huge Air Battles over the Channel', etc., etc. The little man is saying *'Action Stories*, please'. That little man stood for all the drugged millions to whom the world of the gangster and the prize-ring is more 'real', more 'tough', than such things as wars, revolutions, earthquakes, famines and pestilences. From the point of view of a reader of *Action Stories*, a description of the London blitz, or of the struggles of the European underground parties, would be 'sissy stuff'. On the other hand, some puny gun-battle in Chicago, resulting in perhaps half a dozen deaths, would seem genuinely 'tough'. This habit of mind is now extremely widespread. A soldier sprawls in a muddy trench, with the machine-gun bullets crackling a foot or two overhead, and whiles away his intolerable boredom by reading an American gangster story. And what is it that makes that story so exciting? Precisely the fact that people are shooting at each other with machine-guns! Neither the soldier nor anyone else sees anything curious in this. It is taken for granted that an imaginary bullet is more thrilling than a real one.

The obvious explanation is that in real life one is usually a passive victim, whereas in the adventure story one can think of oneself as being at the centre of events. But there is more to it than that. Here it is necessary to refer again to the curious fact of *No Orchids* being written – with technical errors, perhaps, but certainly with considerable skill – in the American language.

There exists in America an enormous literature of more or less the same stamp as *No Orchids*. Quite apart from books, there is the huge array of 'pulp magazines', graded so as to cater for different kinds of fantasy, but nearly all having much the same mental atmosphere. A few of them go in for straight pornography, but the great majority are quite plainly aimed at sadists and masochists. Sold at threepence a copy under the title of Yank Mags,* these things used to enjoy considerable popularity in England, but when the supply dried up owing to the war, no satisfactory substitute was forthcoming. English imitations of the 'pulp magazine' do now exist, but they are poor things compared with the original. English crook films, again, never approach the American crook film in brutality. And yet the career of Mr Chase shows how deep the American influence has already gone. Not only is he himself living a continuous fantasy-life in the Chicago underworld, but he can count on hundreds of thousands of readers who know what is meant by a 'clip-shop' or the 'hotsquat', do not have to do mental arithmetic

* They are said to have been imported into this country as ballast, which accounted for their low price and crumpled appearance. Since the war the ships have been ballasted with something more useful, probably gravel.

when confronted by 'fifty grand', and understand at sight a sentence like 'Johnny was a rummy and only two jumps ahead of the nut-factory'. Evidently there are great numbers of English people who are partly americanized in language and, one ought to add, in moral outlook. For there was no popular protest against *No Orchids*. In the end it was withdrawn, but only retrospectively, when a later work, *Miss Callaghan Comes to Grief*, brought Mr Chase's books to the attention of the authorities. Judging by casual conversations at the time, ordinary readers got a mild thrill out of the obscenities of *No Orchids*, but saw nothing undesirable in the book as a whole. Many people, incidentally, were under the impression that it was an American book reissued in England.

The thing that the ordinary reader *ought* to have objected to – almost certainly would have objected to, a few decades earlier – was the equivocal attitude towards crime. It is implied throughout *No Orchids* that being a criminal is only reprehensible in the sense that it does not pay. Being a policeman pays better, but there is no moral difference, since the police use essentially criminal methods. In a book like *He Won't Need It Now* the distinction between crime and crime-prevention practically disappears. This is a new departure for English sensational fiction, in which till recently there has always been a sharp distinction between right and wrong and a general agreement that virtue must triumph in the last chapter. English books glorifying crime (modern crime, that is – pirates and highwaymen are different) are very rare. Even a book like *Raffles*, as I have pointed out, is governed by powerful taboos, and it is clearly understood that Raffles's crimes must be expiated sooner or later. In America, both in life and fiction, the tendency to tolerate crime, even to admire the criminal so long as he is successful, is very much more marked. It is, indeed, ultimately this attitude that has made it possible for crime to flourish upon so huge a scale. Books have been written about Al Capone that are hardly different in tone from the books written about Henry Ford, Stalin, Lord Northcliffe and all the rest of the 'log cabin to White House' brigade. And switching back eighty years, one finds Mark Twain adopting much the same attitude towards the disgusting bandit Slade, hero of twenty-eight murders, and towards the Western desperadoes generally. They were successful, they 'made good', therefore he admired them.

In a book like *No Orchids* one is not, as in the old-style crime story, simply escaping from dull reality into an imaginary world of action. One's escape is essentially into cruelty and sexual perversion. *No Orchids* is aimed at the power-instinct, which *Raffles* or the Sherlock Holmes stories are not. At the same time the English attitude towards crime is not so superior to the American as I may have seemed to imply. It too is mixed up with power-worship, and has become more noticeably so in the last twenty years. A writer who is worth examining is Edgar Wallace, especially in such typical books as *The Orator* and the Mr J. G. Reeder stories. Wallace was one of the first crime-story writers to break away from the old tradition of the private detective and make his central figure a Scotland Yard official. Sherlock Holmes is an amateur, solving his problems without the help and even, in the earlier stories, against the opposition of the police. Moreover, like Lupin, he is essentially an intellectual, even a scientist. He reasons logically from observed fact, and his intellectuality is constantly contrasted with the routine methods of the police. Wallace objected strongly to this slur, as he considered it, on Scotland Yard, and in several newspaper articles he went out of his way to denounce Holmes by name. His own ideal was the detective-inspector who catches criminals not because he is intellectually brilliant but because he is part of an all-powerful organization. Hence the curious fact that in Wallace's most characteristic stories the 'clue' and the 'deduction' play no part. The criminal is always defeated by an incredible coincidence, or because in some unexplained manner the police know all about the crime beforehand. The tone of the stories makes it quite clear that Wallace's admiration for the police is pure bully-worship. A Scotland Yard detective is the most powerful kind of being that he can imagine, while the criminal figures in his mind as an outlaw against whom anything is permissible, like the condemned slaves in the Roman arena. His policemen behave much more brutally than British policemen do in real life – they hit people without provocation, fire revolvers past their ears to terrify them and so on – and some of the stories exhibit a fearful intellectual sadism. (For instance, Wallace likes to arrange things so that the villain is hanged on the same day as the heroine is married.) But it is sadism after the English fashion: that is to say, it is unconscious, there is not overtly any sex in it, and it keeps within the bounds of the law. The British public tolerates a harsh criminal law and gets a kick out of monstrously unfair murder trials: but still that is better, on any account, than tolerating or admiring crime. If one must worship a bully, it is better that he should be a policeman than a gangster. Wallace is still governed to some extent by the concept of 'not done'. In *No Orchids* anything is 'done' so long as it leads on to power. All the barriers are down, all the motives are out in the open. Chase is a worse symptom than Wallace, to the extent that all-in wrestling is worse than boxing, or Fascism is worse than capitalist democracy.

In borrowing from William Faulkner's *Sanctuary*, Chase only took the plot; the mental atmosphere of the two books is not similar. Chase really derives from other sources, and this particular bit of borrowing is only symbolic. What it symbolizes is the vulgarization of ideas which is constantly happening, and which probably happens faster in an age of print. Chase has been described as 'Faulkner for the masses', but it would be more accurate to describe him as Carlyle for the masses. He is a popular writer – there are many such in America, but they are still rarities in England – who has caught up with what is now fashionable to call 'realism', meaning the doctrine that might is right. The growth of 'realism' has been the great feature of the intellectual history of our own age. Why this should be so is a complicated question. The interconnexion between sadism, masochism, success-worship, power-worship, nationalism, and totalitarianism is a huge subject whose edges have barely been scratched, and even to mention it is considered somewhat indelicate. To take merely the first example that comes to mind, I believe no one has ever pointed out the sadistic and masochistic element in Bernard Shaw's work, still less suggested that this probably has some connexion with Shaw's admiration for dictators. Fascism is often loosely equated with sadism, but nearly always by people who see nothing wrong in the most slavish worship of Stalin. The truth is, of course, that the countless English intellectuals who kiss the arse of Stalin are not different from the minority who give their allegiance to Hitler or Mussolini, nor from the efficiency experts who preached 'punch', 'drive', 'personality' and 'learn to be a Tiger man' in the nineteen-twenties, nor from that older generation of intellectuals, Carlyle, Creasey and the rest of them, who bowed down before German militarism. All of them are worshipping power and successful cruelty. It is important to notice that the cult of power tends to be mixed up with a love of cruelty and wickedness *for their own sakes*. A tyrant is all the more admired if he happens to be a bloodstained crook as well, and 'the end justifies the means' often becomes, in effect, 'the means justify

themselves provided they are dirty enough'. This idea
colours the outlook of all sympathizers with totalitarianism,
and accounts, for instance, for the positive delight with
which many English intellectuals greeted the Nazi-Soviet
pact. It was a step only doubtfully useful to the U.S.S.R.,
but it was entirely unmoral, and for that reason to be admired; the explanations of it, which were numerous and
self-contradictory, could come afterwards.

Until recently the characteristic adventure stories of the
English-speaking peoples have been stories in which the
hero fights *against odds*. This is true all the way from Robin
Hood to Pop-eye the Sailor. Perhaps the basic myth of the
Western world is Jack the Giant-killer, but to be brought
up to date this should be renamed Jack the Dwarf-killer, and
there already exists a considerable literature which teaches,
either overtly or implicitly, that one should side with the big
man against the little man. Most of what is now written
about foreign policy is simply an embroidery on this theme,
and for several decades such phrases as 'Play the game',
'Don't hit a man when he's down' and 'It's not cricket'
have never failed to draw a snigger from anyone of intellectual pretensions. What is comparatively new is to find the
accepted pattern, according to which (*a*) right is right and
wrong is wrong, whoever wins, and (*b*) weakness must be
respected, disappearing from popular literature as well.
When I first read D. H. Lawrence's novels, at the age of
about twenty, I was puzzled by the fact that there did not
seem to be any classification of the characters into 'good' and
'bad'. Lawrence seemed to sympathize with all of them
about equally, and this was so unusual as to give me the
feeling of having lost my bearings. Today no one would
think of looking for heroes and villains in a serious novel,
but in lowbrow fiction one still expects to find a sharp distinction between right and wrong and between legality and

illegality. The common people, on the whole, are still living in the world of absolute good and evil from which the intellectuals have long since escaped. But the popularity of *No Orchids* and the American books and magazines to which it is akin shows how rapidly the doctrine of 'realism' is gaining ground.

Several people, after reading *No Orchids*, have remarked to me, 'It's pure Fascism'. This is a correct description, although the book has not the smallest connexion with politics and very little with social or economic problems. It has merely the same relation to Fascism as, say Trollope's novels have to nineteenth-century capitalism. It is a daydream appropriate to a totalitarian age. In his imagined world of gangsters Chase is presenting, as it were, a distilled version of the modern political scene, in which such things as mass bombing of civilians, the use of hostages, torture to obtain confessions, secret prisons, execution without trial, floggings with rubber truncheons, drownings in cesspools, systematic falsification of records and statistics, treachery, bribery, and quislingism are normal and morally neutral, even admirable when they are done in a large and bold way. The average man is not directly interested in politics, and when he reads, he wants the current struggles of the world to be translated into a simple story about individuals. He can take an interest in Slim and Fenner as he could not in the G.P.U. and the Gestapo. People worship power in the form in which they are able to understand it. A twelve-year-old boy worships Jack Dempsey. An adolescent in a Glasgow slum worships Al Capone. An aspiring pupil at a business college worships Lord Nuffield. A *New Statesman* reader worships Stalin. There is a difference in intellectual maturity, but none in moral outlook. Thirty years ago the heroes of popular fiction had nothing in common with Mr Chase's gangsters and detectives, and the idols of the English liberal intelligentsia were also comparatively sympathetic figures. Between Holmes and Fenner on the one hand, and between Abraham Lincoln and Stalin on the other, there is a similar gulf.

One ought not to infer too much from the success of Mr Chase's books. It is possible that it is an isolated phenomenon, brought about by the mingled boredom and brutality of war. But if such books should definitely acclimatize themselves in England, instead of being merely a half-understood import from America, there would be good grounds for dismay. In choosing *Raffles* as a background for *No Orchids* I deliberately chose a book which by the standards of its time was morally equivocal. Raffles, as I have pointed out, has no real moral code, no religion, certainly no social consciousness. All he has is a set of reflexes – the nervous system, as it were, of a gentleman. Give him a sharp tap on this reflex or that (they are called 'sport', 'pal', 'woman', 'king and country' and so forth), and you get a predictable reaction. In Mr Chase's books there are no gentlemen and no taboos. Emancipation is complete. Freud and Machiavelli have reached the outer suburbs. Comparing the schoolboy atmosphere of the one book with the cruelty and corruption of the other, one is driven to feel that snobbishness, like hypocrisy, is a check upon behaviour whose value from a social point of view has been underrated.

1944

Charles Dickens

I

Dickens is one of those writers who are well worth stealing. Even the burial of his body in Westminster Abbey was a species of theft, if you come to think of it.

When Chesterton wrote his introductions to the Everyman Edition of Dickens's works, it seemed quite natural to him to credit Dickens with his own highly individual brand of medievalism, and more recently a Marxist writer, Mr T. A. Jackson, has made spirited efforts to turn Dickens into a blood-thirsty revolutionary. The Marxist claims him as 'almost' a Marxist, the Catholic claims him as 'almost' a Catholic, and both claim him as a champion of the proletariat (or 'the poor', as Chesterton would have put it). On the other hand, Nadezhda Krupskaya, in her little book on Lenin, relates that towards the end of his life Lenin went to see a dramatized version of *The Cricket on the Hearth*, and found Dickens's 'middle-class sentimentality' so intolerable that he walked out in the middle of a scene.

Taking 'middle-class' to mean what Krupskaya might be expected to mean by it, this was probably a truer judgement than those of Chesterton and Jackson. But it is worth noticing that the dislike of Dickens implied in this remark is something unusual. Plenty of people have found him unreadable, but very few seem to have felt any hostility towards the general spirit of his work. Some years later Mr Bechhofer Roberts published a full-length attack on Dickens in the form of a novel (*This Side Idolatry*), but it was a merely personal attack, concerned for the most part with Dickens's treatment of his wife. It dealt with incidents which not one in a thousand of Dickens's readers would ever hear about, and which no more invalidates his work than the second-best bed invalidates *Hamlet*. All that the book really demonstrated was that a writer's literary personality has little or nothing to do with his private character. It is quite possible that in private life Dickens was just the kind of insensitive egoist that Mr Bechhofer Roberts makes him appear. But in his published work there is implied a personality quite different from this, a personality which has won him far more friends than enemies. It might well have been otherwise, for even if Dickens was a bourgeois, he was certainly a subversive writer, a radical, one might truthfully say a rebel. Everyone who has read widely in his work has felt this. Gissing, for instance, the best of the writers on Dickens, was anything but a radical himself, and he disapproved of this strain in Dickens and wished it were not there, but it never occurred to him to deny it. In *Oliver Twist, Hard Times, Bleak House, Little Dorrit*, Dickens attacked English institutions with a ferocity that has never since been approached. Yet he managed to do it without making himself hated, and, more than this, the very people he attacked have swallowed him so completely that he has become a national institution himself. In its attitude towards Dickens the English public has always been a little like the elephant which feels a blow with a walking-stick as a delightful tickling. Before I was ten years old I was having Dickens ladled down my throat by schoolmasters in whom even at that age I could see a strong resemblance to Mr Creakle, and one knows without needing to be told that lawyers delight in Sergeant Buzfuz and that *Little Dorrit* is a favourite in the Home Office. Dickens seems to have succeeded in attacking everybody and antagonizing nobody. Naturally this makes one wonder whether after all there was something unreal in his attack upon society. Where exactly does he stand, socially, morally, and politically? As usual, one can define his position more easily if one starts by deciding what he was *not*.

In the first place he was *not*, as Messrs Chesterton and Jackson seem to imply, a 'proletarian' writer. To begin with, he does not write about the proletariat, in which he merely resembles the overwhelming majority of novelists, past and present. If you look for the working classes in fiction, and especially English fiction, all you find is a hole. This statement needs qualifying, perhaps. For reasons that are easy enough to see, the agricultural labourer (in England a proletarian) gets a fairly good showing in fiction, and a great deal has been written about criminals, derelicts and, more recently, the working-class intelligentsia. But the ordinary town proletariat, the people who make the wheels go round, have always been ignored by novelists. When they do find their way between the covers of a book, it is nearly always as objects of pity or as comic relief. The central action of Dickens's stories almost invariably takes place in middle-class surroundings. If one examines his novels in detail one finds that his real subject-matter is the London commercial bourgeoisie and their hangers-on – lawyers, clerks, tradesmen, innkeepers, small craftsmen, and servants. He has no portrait of an agricultural worker, and only one (Stephen Blackpool in *Hard Times*) of an industrial worker. The Plornishes in *Little Dorrit* are probably his best picture of a working-class family – the Peggottys, for instance, hardly belong to the working class – but on the whole he is not successful with this type of character. If you ask any ordinary reader which of Dickens's proletarian characters he can remember, the three he is almost certain to mention are Bill Sykes, Sam Weller, and Mrs Gamp. A burglar, a valet, and a drunken midwife – not exactly a representative cross-section of the English working class.

Secondly, in the ordinarily accepted sense of the word, Dickens is not a 'revolutionary' writer. But his position here needs some defining.

Whatever else Dickens may have been, he was not a hole-and-corner soul-saver, the kind of well-meaning idiot who thinks that the world will be perfect if you amend a few by-laws and abolish a few anomalies. It is worth comparing him with Charles Reade, for instance. Reade was a much better-informed man than Dickens, and in some ways more public-spirited. He really hated the abuses he could understand, he showed them up in a series of novels which for all their absurdity are extremely readable, and he probably helped to alter public opinion on a few minor but important points. But it was quite beyond him to grasp that, given the existing form of society, certain evils *cannot* be remedied. Fasten upon this or that minor abuse, expose it, drag it into the open, bring it before a British jury, and all will be well – that is how he sees it. Dickens at any rate never imagined that you can cure pimples by cutting them off. In every page of his work one can see a consciousness that society is wrong somewhere at the root. It is when one asks 'Which root?' that one begins to grasp his position.

The truth is that Dickens's criticism of society is almost exclusively moral. Hence the utter lack of any constructive suggestion anywhere in his work. He attacks the law, parliamentary government, the educational system and so forth, without ever clearly suggesting what he would put in their places. Of course it is not necessarily the business of a novelist, or a satirist, to make constructive suggestions, but the point is that Dickens's attitude is at bottom not even destructive. There is no clear sign that he wants the existing order to be overthrown, or that he believes it would make very much difference if it *were* overthrown. For in reality his target is not so much society as 'human nature'. It would be difficult to point anywhere in his books to a passage suggesting that the economic system is wrong *as a system*. Nowhere, for instance, does he make any attack on private enterprise or private property. Even in a book like *Our Mutual Friend*, which turns on the power of corpses to interfere with living people by means of idiotic wills, it does not occur to him to suggest that individuals ought not to have this irresponsible power. Of course one can draw this inference for oneself, and one can draw it again from the remarks about Bounderby's will at the end of *Hard Times*, and indeed from the whole of Dickens's work one can infer the evil of *laissez-faire* capitalism; but Dickens makes no such inference himself. It is said that Macaulay refused to review *Hard Times* because he disapproved of its 'sullen Socialism'. Obviously Macaulay is here using the word 'Socialism' in the same sense in which, twenty years ago, a vegetarian meal or a Cubist picture used to be referred to as 'Bolshevism'. There is not a line in the book that can properly be called Socialistic; indeed, its tendency if anything is pro-capitalist, because its whole moral is that capitalists ought to be kind, not that workers ought to be rebellious. Bounderby is a bullying windbag and Gradgrind has been morally blinded, but if they were better men, the system would work well enough – that, all through, is the implication. And so far as social criticism goes, one can never extract much more from Dickens than this, unless one deliberately reads meanings into him. His whole 'message' is one that at first glance looks like an enormous platitude : If men would behave decently the world would be decent.

Naturally this calls for a few characters who are in positions of authority and who *do* behave decently. Hence that recurrent Dickens figure, the good rich man. This character belongs especially to Dickens's early optimistic period.

He is usually a 'merchant' (we are not necessarily told what merchandise he deals in), and he is always a superhumanly kind-hearted old gentleman who 'trots' to and fro, raising his employees' wages, patting children on the head, getting debtors out of jail and in general, acting the fairy godmother. Of course he is a pure dream figure, much further from real life than, say, Squeers or Micawber. Even Dickens must have reflected occasionally that anyone who was so anxious to give his money away would never have acquired it in the first place. Mr Pickwick, for instance, had 'been in the city', but it is difficult to imagine him making a fortune there. Nevertheless this character runs like a connecting thread through most of the earlier books. Pickwick, the Cheerybles, old Chuzzlewit, Scrooge – it is the same figure over and over again, the good rich man, handing out guineas. Dickens does however show signs of development here. In the books of the middle period the good rich man fades out to some extent. There is no one who plays this part in *A Tale of Two Cities*, nor in *Great Expectations* – *Great Expectations* is, in fact, definitely an attack on patronage– and in *Hard Times* it is only very doubtfully played by Gradgrind after his reformation. The character reappears in a rather different form as Meagles in *Little Dorrit* and John Jarndyce in *Bleak House* – one might perhaps add Betsy Trotwood in *David Copperfield*. But in these books the good rich man has dwindled from a 'merchant' to a rentier. This is significant. A rentier is part of the possessing class, he can and, almost without knowing it, does make other people work for him, but he has very little direct power. Unlike Scrooge or the Cheerybles, he cannot put everything right by raising everybody's wages. The seeming inference from the rather despondent books that Dickens wrote in the fifties is that by that time he had grasped the helplessness of well-meaning individuals in a corrupt society. Nevertheless in the last completed novel, *Our Mutual Friend* (published 1864–5), the good rich man comes back in full glory in the person of Boffin. Boffin is a proletarian by origin and only rich by inheritance, but he is the usual *deus ex machina*, solving everybody's problems by showering money in all directions. He even 'trots', like the Cheerybles. In several ways *Our Mutual Friend* is a return to the earlier manner, and not an unsuccessful return either. Dickens's thoughts seem to have come full circle. Once again, individual kindliness is the remedy for everything.

One crying evil of his time that Dickens says very little about is child labour. There are plenty of pictures of suffering children in his books, but usually they are suffering in schools rather than in factories. The one detailed account of child labour that he gives is the description in *David Copperfield* of little David washing bottles in Murdstone & Grinby's warehouse. This, of course, is autobiography. Dickens himself, at the age of ten, had worked in Warren's blacking factory in the Strand, very much as he describes it here. It was a terribly bitter memory to him, partly because he felt the whole incident to be discreditable to his parents, and he even concealed it from his wife till long after they were married. Looking back on this period, he says in *David Copperfield*:

It is a matter of some surprise to me, even now, that I can have been so easily thrown away at such an age. A child of excellent abilities and with strong powers of observation, quick, eager, delicate, and soon hurt bodily or mentally, it seems wonderful to me that nobody should have made any sign in my behalf. But none was made; and I became, at ten years old, a little labouring hind in the service of Murdstone & Grinby.

And again, having described the rough boys among whom he worked:

No words can express the secret agony of my soul as I sunk into this companionship ... and felt my hopes of growing up to be a learned and distinguished man crushed in my bosom.

Obviously it is not David Copperfield who is speaking, it is Dickens himself. He uses almost the same words in the autobiography that he began and abandoned a few months earlier. Of course Dickens is right in saying that a gifted child ought not to work ten hours a day pasting labels on bottles, but what he does not say is that *no* child ought to be condemned to such a fate, and there is no reason for inferring that he thinks it. David escapes from the warehouse, but Mick Walker and Mealy Potatoes and the others are still there, and there is no sign that this troubles Dickens particularly. As usual, he displays no consciousness that the *structure* of society can be changed. He despises politics, does not believe that any good can come out of Parliament – he had been a Parliamentary shorthand writer, which was no doubt a disillusioning experience – and he is slightly hostile to the most hopeful movement of his day, trade unionism. In *Hard Times* trade unionism is represented as something not much better than a racket, something that happens because employers are not sufficiently paternal. Stephen Blackpool's refusal to join the union is rather a virtue in Dickens's eyes. Also, as Mr Jackson has pointed out, the apprentices' association in *Barnaby Rudge*, to which Sim Tappertit belongs, is probably a hit at the illegal or barely legal unions of Dickens's own day, with their secret assemblies, passwords and so forth. Obviously he wants the workers to be decently treated, but there is no sign that he wants them to take their destiny into their own hands, least of all by open violence.

As it happens, Dickens deals with revolution in the narrower sense in two novels, *Barnaby Rudge* and *A Tale of Two Cities*. In *Barnaby Rudge* it is a case of rioting rather than revolution. The Gordon Riots of 1780, though they had religious bigotry as a pretext, seem to have been little more than a pointless outburst of looting. Dickens's attitude to this kind of thing is sufficiently indicated by the fact that his first idea was to make the ringleaders of the riots three lunatics escaped from an asylum. He was dissuaded from this, but the principal figure of the book is in fact a village idiot. In the chapters dealing with the riots Dickens shows a most profound horror of mob violence. He delights in describing scenes in which the 'dregs' of the population behave with atrocious bestiality. These chapters are of great psychological interest, because they show how deeply he had brooded on this subject. The things he describes can only have come out of his imagination, for no riots on anything like the same scale had happened in his lifetime. Here is one of his descriptions, for instance :

If Bedlam gates had been flung open wide, there would not have issued forth such maniacs as the frenzy of that night had made. There were men there who danced and trampled on the beds of flowers as though they trod down human enemies, and wrenched them from their stalks, like savages who twisted human necks. There were men who cast their lighted torches in the air, and suffered them to fall upon their heads and faces, blistering the skin with deep unseemly burns. There were men who rushed up to the fire, and paddled in it with their hands as if in water; and others who were restrained by force from plunging in, to gratify their deadly longing. On the skull of one drunken lad – not twenty, by his looks – who lay upon the ground with a bottle to his mouth, the lead from the roof came streaming down in a shower of liquid fire, white hot, melting his head like wax. . . . But of all the howling throng not one learnt mercy from, or sickened at, these sights; nor was the fierce, besotted, senseless rage of one man glutted.

You might almost think you were reading a description

of 'Red' Spain by a partisan of General Franco. One ought, of course, to remember that when Dickens was writing, the London 'mob' still existed. (Nowadays there is no mob, only a flock.) Low wages and the growth and shift of population had brought into existence a huge, dangerous slum-proletariat, and until the early middle of the nineteen century there was hardly such a thing as a police force. When the brickbats began to fly there was nothing between shuttering your windows and ordering the troops to open fire. In *A Tale of Two Cities* he is dealing with a revolution which was really *about* something, and Dickens's attitude is different, but not entirely different. As a matter of fact, *A Tale of Two Cities* is a book which tends to leave a false impression behind, especially after a lapse of time.

The one thing that everyone who has read *A Tale of Two Cities* remembers is the Reign of Terror. The whole book is dominated by the guillotine – tumbrils thundering to and fro, bloody knives, heads bouncing into the basket, and sinister old women knitting as they watch. Actually these scenes only occupy a few chapters, but they are written with terrible intensity, and the rest of the book is rather slow going. But *A Tale of Two Cities* is not a companion volume to *The Scarlet Pimpernel*. Dickens sees clearly enough that the French Revolution was bound to happen and that many of the people who were executed deserved what they got. If, he says, you behave as the French aristocracy had behaved, vengeance will follow. He repeats this over and over again. We are constantly being reminded that while 'my lord' is lolling in bed, with four liveried footmen serving his chocolate and the peasants starving outside, somewhere in the forest a tree is growing which will presently be sawn into planks for the platform of the guillotine, etc., etc., etc. The inevitability of the Terror, given its causes, is insisted upon in the clearest terms :

It was too much the way ... to talk of this terrible Revolution as if it were the only harvest ever known under the skies that had not been sown – as if nothing had ever been done, or omitted to be done, that had led to it – as if observers of the wretched millions in France, and of the misused and perverted resources that should have made them prosperous, had not seen it inevitably coming, years before, and had not in plain terms recorded what they saw.

And again:

All the devouring and insatiate monsters imagined since imagination could record itself, are fused in the one realization, Guillotine. And yet there is not in France, with its rich variety of soil and climate, a blade, a leaf, a root, a spring, a peppercorn, which will grow to maturity under conditions more certain than those that have produced this horror. Crush humanity out of shape once more, under similar hammers, and it will twist itself into the same tortured forms.

In other words, the French aristocracy had dug their own graves. But there is no perception here of what is now called historic necessity. Dickens sees that the results are inevitable, given the causes, but he thinks that the causes might have been avoided. The Revolution is something that happens because centuries of oppression have made the French peasantry sub-human. If the wicked nobleman could somehow have turned over a new leaf, like Scrooge, there would have been no Revolution, no jacquerie, no guillotine – and so much the better. This is the opposite of the 'revolutionary' attitude. From the 'revolutionary' point of view the class-struggle is the main source of progress, and therefore the nobleman who robs the peasant and goads him to revolt is playing a necessary part, just as much as the Jacobin who guillotines the nobleman. Dickens never writes anywhere a line that can be interpreted as meaning this. Revolution as he sees it is merely a monster that is begotten by tyranny and always ends by devouring its own instruments. In Sydney Carton's vision at the foot of the guillotine, he foresees Defarge and the other leading spirits of the Terror all perishing under the same knife – which, in fact, was approximately what happened.

And Dickens is very sure that revolution *is* a monster. That is why everyone remembers the revolutionary scenes in *A Tale of Two Cities*; they have the quality of nightmare, and it is Dickens's own nightmare. Again and again he insists upon the meaningless horrors of revolution – the mass-butcheries, the injustice, the ever-present terror of spies, the frightful blood-lust of the mob. The descriptions of the Paris mob – the description, for instance, of the crowd of murderers struggling round the grindstone to sharpen their weapons before butchering the prisoners in the September massacres – outdo anything in *Barnaby Rudge*. The revolutionaries appear to him simply as degraded savages – in fact, as lunatics. He broods over their frenzies with a curious imaginative intensity. He describes them dancing the 'Carmagnole', for instance:

There could not be fewer than five hundred people, and they were dancing like five thousand demons.... They danced to the popular Revolution song, keeping a ferocious time that was like a gnashing of teeth in unison.... They advanced, retreated, struck at one another's hands, clutched at one another's heads, spun round alone, caught one another, and spun around in pairs, until many of them dropped.... Suddenly they stopped again, paused, struck out the time afresh, forming into lines the width of the public way, and, with their heads low down and their hands high up, swooped screaming off. No fight could have been half so terrible as this dance. It was so emphatically a fallen sport – a something, once innocent, delivered over to all devilry.

He even credits some of these wretches with a taste for guillotining children. The passage I have abridged above ought to be read in full. It and others like it show how deep was Dickens's horror of revolutionary hysteria. Notice, for instance that touch, 'with their heads low down and their hands high up', etc., and the evil vision it conveys. Madame Defarge is a truly dreadful figure, certainly Dickens's most successful attempt at a *malignant* character. Defarge and others are simply 'the new oppressors who have risen in the destruction of the old', the revolutionary courts are presided over by 'the lowest, cruellest and worst populace', and so on and so forth. All the way through Dickens insists upon the nightmare insecurity of a revolutionary period, and in this he shows a great deal of prescience. 'A law of the suspected, which struck away all security for liberty or life, and delivered over any good and innocent person to any bad and guilty one; prisons gorged with people who had committed no offence, and could obtain no hearing' – it would apply pretty accurately to several countries today.

The apologists of any revolution generally try to minimize its horrors; Dickens's impulse is to exaggerate them – and from a historical point of view he has certainly exaggerated. Even the Reign of Terror was a much smaller thing than he makes it appear. Though he quotes no figures, he gives the impression of a frenzied massacre lasting for years, whereas in reality the whole of the Terror, so far as the number of deaths goes, was a joke compared with one of Napoleon's battles. But the bloody knives and the tumbrils rolling to and fro create in his mind a special sinister vision which he has succeeded in passing on to generations of readers. Thanks to Dickens, the very word 'tumbril' has a murderous sound; one forgets that a tumbril is only a sort of farm-cart. To this day, to the average Englishman, the French Revolution means no more than a pyramid of severed heads. It is a strange thing that Dickens, much more in sympathy with the ideas of the Revolution than most Englishmen of his time, should have played a part in creating this impression.

If you hate violence and don't believe in politics, the only remedy remaining is education. Perhaps society is past praying for, but there is always hope for the individual human being, if you can catch him young enough. This belief partly accounts for Dickens's preoccupation with childhoood.

No one, at any rate no English writer, has written better about childhood than Dickens. In spite of all the knowledge that has accumulated since, in spite of the fact that children are now comparatively sanely treated, no novelist has shown the same power of entering into the child's point of view. I must have been about nine years old when I first read *David Copperfield*. The mental atmosphere of the opening chapters was so immediately intelligible to me that I vaguely imagined they had been written *by a child*. And yet when one re-reads the book as an adult and sees the Murdstones, for instance, dwindle from gigantic figures of doom into semi-comic monsters, these passages lose nothing. Dickens has been able to stand both inside and outside the child's mind, in such a way that the same scene can be wild burlesque or sinister reality, according to the age at which one reads it. Look, for instance, at the scene in which David Copperfield is unjustly suspected of eating the mutton chops; or the scene in which Pip, in *Great Expectations*, coming back from Miss Havisham's house and finding himself completely unable to describe what he has seen, takes refuge in a series of outrageous lies – which, of course, are eagerly believed. All the isolation of childhood is there. And how accurately he has recorded the mechanisms of the child's mind, its visualizing tendency, its sensitiveness to certain kinds of impression. Pip relates how in his childhood his ideas about his dead parents were derived from their tombstones :

The shape of the letters on my father's, gave me an odd idea that he was a square, stout, dark man, with curly black hair.

From the character and turn of the inscription, 'ALSO GEORG-
IANA, WIFE OF THE ABOVE', I drew a childish conclusion that
my mother was freckled and sickly. To five little stone lozenges,
each about a foot and a half long, which were arranged in a neat
row beside their grave, and were sacred to the memory of five
little brothers of mine … I am indebted for a belief I religiously
entertained that they had all been born on their backs with their
hands in their trouser-pockets, and had never taken them out in
this state of existence.

There is a similar passage in *David Copperfield*. After
biting Mr Murdstone's hand, David is sent away to school
and obliged to wear on his back a placard saying, 'Take care
of him. He bites.' He looks at the door in the playground
where the boys have carved their names, and from the appearance of each name he seems to know in just what tone
of voice the boy will read out the placard :

There was one boy – a certain J. Steerforth – who cut his
name very deep and very often, who, I conceived, would read
it in a rather strong voice, and afterwards pull my hair. There
was another boy, one Tommy Traddles, who I dreaded would
make game of it, and pretend to be dreadfully frightened of me.
There was a third, George Demple, who I fancied would sing it.

When I read this passage as a child, it seemed to me that
those were exactly the pictures that those particular names
would call up. The reason, of course, is the sound-associa-
tions of the words Demple ('temple'; Traddles – probably
'skedaddle'). But how many people, before Dickens, had
ever noticed such things ? A sympathetic attitude towards
children was a much rarer thing in Dicken's day than it is
now. The early nineteenth century was not a good time to
be a child. In Dickens's youth children were still being
'solemnly tried at a criminal bar, where they were held up
to be seen', and it was not so long since boys of thirteen had
been hanged for petty theft. The doctrine of 'breaking the

child's spirit' was in full vigour, and *The Fairchild Family* was a standard book for children till late into the century. This evil book is now issued in pretty-pretty expurgated editions, but it is well worth reading in the original version. It gives one some idea of the lengths to which child-discipline was sometimes carried. Mr Fairchild, for instance, when he catches his children quarrelling, first thrashes them, reciting Dr Watts's 'Let dogs delight to bark and bite' between blows of the cane, and then takes them to spend the afternoon beneath a gibbet where the rotting corpse of a murderer is hanging. In the earlier part of the century scores of thousands of children, aged sometimes as young as six, were literally worked to death in the mines or cotton mills, and even at the fashionable public schools boys were flogged till they ran with blood for a mistake in their Latin verses. One thing which Dickens seems to have recognized, and which most of his contemporaries did not, is the sadistic sexual element in flogging. I think this can be inferred from *David Copperfield* and *Nicholas Nickleby*. But mental cruelty to a child infuriates him as much as physical, and though there is a fair number of exceptions, his schoolmasters are generally scoundrels.

Except for the universities and the big public schools, every kind of education then existing in England gets a mauling at Dickens's hands. There is Doctor Blimber's Academy, where little boys are blown up with Greek until they burst, and the revolting charity schools of the period, which produced specimens like Noah Claypole and Uriah Heep, and Salem House, and Dotheboys Hall, and the disgraceful little dame-school kept by Mr Wopsle's great-aunt. Some of what Dickens says remains true even today. Salem House is the ancestor of the modern 'prep school', which still has a good deal of resemblance to it; and as for Mr Wopsle's great-aunt, some old fraud of much the same stamp is carrying on at this moment in nearly every small town in England. But, as usual, Dickens's criticism is neither creative nor destructive. He sees the idiocy of an educational system founded on the Greek lexicon and the wax-ended cane; on the other hand, he has no use for the new kind of school that is coming up in the fifties and sixties, the 'modern' school, with its gritty insistence on 'facts'. What, then, *does* he want? As always, what he appears to want is a moralized version of the existing thing – the old type of school, but with no caning, no bullying or underfeeding, and not quite so much Greek. Doctor Strong's school, to which David Copperfield goes after he escapes from Murdstone & Grinby's, is simply Salem House with the vices left out and a good deal of 'old grey stones' atmosphere thrown in:

Doctor Strong's was an excellent school, as different from Mr Creakle's as good is from evil. It was very gravely and decorously ordered, and on a sound system; with an appeal, in everything, to the honour and good faith of the boys ... which worked wonders. We all felt that we had a part in the management of the place, and in sustaining its character and dignity. Hence, we soon became warmly attached to it – I am sure I did for one, and I never knew, in all my time, of any boy being otherwise – and learnt with a good will, desiring to do it credit. We had noble games out of hours, and plenty of liberty; but even then, as I remember, we were well spoken of in the town, and rarely did any disgrace, by our appearance or manner, to the reputation of Doctor Strong and Doctor Strong's boys.

In the woolly vagueness of this passage one can see Dickens's utter lack of any educational theory. He can imagine the *moral* atmosphere of a good school, but nothing further. The boys 'learnt with a good will', but what did they learn? No doubt it was Doctor Blimber's curriculum, a little watered down. Considering the attitude to society that is everywhere implied in Dickens's novels, it comes as rather a shock to learn that he sent his eldest son to Eton and sent all his children through the ordinary educational mill. Gissing seems to think that he may have done this because he was painfully conscious of being under-educated himself. Here perhaps Gissing is influenced by his own love of classical learning. Dickens had had little or no formal education, but he lost nothing by missing it, and on the whole he seems to have been aware of this. If he was unable to imagine a better school than Doctor Strong's, or, in real life, than Eton, it was probably due to an intellectual deficiency rather different from the one Gissing suggests.

It seems that in every attack Dickens makes upon society he is always pointing to a change of spirit rather than a change of structure. It is hopeless to try and pin him down to any definite remedy, still more to any political doctrine. His approach is always along the moral plane, and his attitude is sufficiently summed up in that remark about Strong's school being as different from Creakle's 'as good is from evil'. Two things can be very much alike and yet abysmally different. Heaven and Hell are in the same place. Useless to change institutions without a 'change of heart' – that, essentially, is what he is always saying.

If that were all, he might be no more than a cheer-up writer, a reactionary humbug. A 'change of heart' is in fact *the* alibi of people who do not wish to endanger the *status quo*. But Dickens is not a humbug, except in minor matters, and the strongest single impression one carries away from his books is that of a hatred of tyranny. I said earlier that Dickens is not *in the accepted sense* a revolutionary writer. But it is not at all certain that a merely moral criticism of society may not be just as 'revolutionary' – and revolution, after all, means turning things upside down – as the politico-economic criticism which is fashionable at this moment. Blake was not a politician, but there is more

97

understanding of the nature of capitalist society in a poem like 'I wander through each charted street' than in three-quarters of Socialist literature. Progress is not an illusion, it happens, but it is slow and invariably disappointing. There is always a new tyrant waiting to take over from the old – generally not quite so bad, but still a tyrant. Consequently two viewpoints are always tenable. The one, how can you improve human nature until you have changed the system? The other, what is the use of changing the system before you have improved human nature? They appeal to different individuals, and they probably show a tendency to alternate in point of time. The moralist and the revolutionary are constantly undermining one another. Marx exploded a hundred tons of dynamite beneath the moralist position, and we are still living in the echo of that tremendous crash. But already, somewhere or other, the sappers are at work and fresh dynamite is being tamped in place to blow Marx at the moon. Then Marx, or somebody like him, will come back with yet more dynamite, and so the process continues, to an end we cannot yet foresee. The central problem – how to prevent power from being abused – remains unsolved. Dickens, who had not the vision to see that private property is an obstructive nuisance, had the vision to see that. 'If men would behave decently the world would be decent' is not such a platitude as it sounds.

II

More completely than most writers, perhaps, Dickens can be explained in terms of his social origin, though actually his family history was not quite what one would infer from his novels. His father was a clerk in government service, and through his mother's family he had connexions with both the Army and the Navy. But from the age of nine onwards he was brought up in London in commercial surroundings, and generally in an atmosphere of struggling poverty. Mentally he belongs to the small urban bourgeoisie, and he happens to be an exceptionally fine specimen of this class, with all the 'points', as it were, very highly developed. That is partly what makes him so interesting. If one wants a modern equivalent, the nearest would be H. G. Wells, who has had a rather similar history and who obviously owes something to Dickens as novelist. Arnold Bennett was essentially of the same type, but, unlike the other two, he was a midlander, with an industrial and noncomformist rather than commercial and Anglican background.

The great disadvantage, and advantage, of the small urban bourgeois is his limited outlook. He sees the world as a middle-class world, and everything outside these limits is either laughable or slightly wicked. On the one hand, he has no contact with industry or the soil; on the other, no contact with the governing classes. Anyone who has studied Wells's novels in detail will have noticed that though he hates the aristocrat like poison, he has no particular objection to the plutocrat, and no enthusiasm for the proletarian. His most hated types, the people he believes to be responsible for all human ills, are kings, landowners, priests, nationalists, soldiers, scholars and peasants. At first sight a list beginning with kings and ending with peasants looks like a mere omnium gatherum, but in reality all these people have a common factor. All of them are archaic types, people who are governed by tradition and whose eyes are turned towards the past – the opposite, therefore, of the rising bourgeois who has put his money on the future and sees the past simply as a dead hand.

Actually, although Dickens lived in a period when the bourgeoisie was really a rising class, he displays this characteristic less strongly than Wells. He is almost unconscious of the future and has a rather sloppy love of the picturesque (the 'quaint old church', etc). Nevertheless his list of most hated types is like enough to Wells's for the similarity to be striking. He is vaguely on the side of the working class – has a sort of generalized sympathy with them because they are oppressed – but he does not in reality know much about them; they come into his books chiefly as servants, and comic servants at that. At the other end of the scale he loathes the aristocrat and – going one better than Wells in this – loathes the big bourgeois as well. His real sympathies are bounded by Mr Pickwick on the upper side and Mr Barkis on the lower. But the term 'aristocrat', for the type Dickens hates, is vague and needs defining.

Actually Dickens's target is not so much the great aristocracy, who hardly enter into his books, as their petty offshoots, the cadging dowagers who live up mews in Mayfair, and the bureaucrats and professional soldiers. All through his books there are countless hostile sketches of these people, and hardly any that are friendly. There are practically no friendly pictures of the landowning class, for instance. One might make a doubtful exception of Sir Leicester Dedlock; otherwise there is only Mr Wardle (who is a stock figure – the 'good old squire') and Haredale in *Barnaby Rudge*, who has Dickens's sympathy because he is a persecuted Catholic. There are no friendly pictures of soldiers (i.e. officers), and none at all of naval men. As for his bureaucrats, judges and magistrates, most of them would feel quite at home in the Circumlocution Office. The only officials whom Dickens handles with any kind of friendliness are, significantly enough, policemen.

Dickens's attitude is easily intelligible to an Englishman, because it is part of the English puritan tradition, which is not dead even at this day. The class Dickens belonged to, at least by adoption, was growing suddenly rich after a couple of centuries of obscurity. It had grown up mainly in the big towns, out of contact with agriculture, and politically impotent; government, in its experience, was something which either interfered or persecuted. Consequently it was a class with no tradition of public service and not much tradition of usefulness. What now strikes us as remarkable about the new moneyed class of the nineteenth century is their complete irresponsibility; they see everything in terms of individual success, with hardly any consciousness that the community exists. On the other hand, a Tite Barnacle, even when he was neglecting his duties, would have some vague notion of what duties he was neglecting. Dickens's attitude is never irresponsible, still less does he take the money-grubbing Smilesian line; but at the back of his mind there is usually a half-belief that the whole apparatus of government is unnecessary. Parliament is simply Lord Coodle and Sir Thomas Doodle, the Empire is simply Major Bagstock and his Indian servant, the Army is simply Colonel Chowser and Doctor Slammer, the public services are simply Bumble and the Circumlocution Office – and so on and so forth. What he does not see, or only intermittently sees, is that Coodle and Doodle and all the other corpses left over from the eighteenth century *are* performing a function which neither Pickwick nor Boffin would ever bother about.

And of course this narrowness of vision is in one way a great advantage to him, because it is fatal for a caricaturist to see too much. From Dickens's point of view 'good' society is simply a collection of village idiots. What a crew! Lady Tippins! Mrs Gowan! Lord Verisopht! The Honourable Bob Stables! Mrs Sparsit (whose husband was a Powler)! The Tite Barnacles! Nupkins! It is practically a case-book in lunacy. But at the same time his remoteness from the land-owning-military-bureaucratic class incapacitates him for full-length satire. He only succeeds with this class when he depicts them as mental defectives. The accusation which used to be made against Dickens in his lifetime, that he 'could not paint a gentleman', was an absurdity, but it is true in this sense, that what he says against the 'gentleman' class is seldom very damaging. Sir Mulberry Hawk, for instance, is a wretched attempt at the wicked-baronet type. Harthouse in *Hard Times* is better, but he would be only an ordinary achievement for Trollope or Thackeray. Trollope's thoughts hardly move outside the 'gentleman' class, but Thackeray has the great advantage of having a foot in two moral camps. In some ways his outlook is very similar to Dickens's. Like Dickens, he identifies with the puritanical moneyed class against the card-playing, debt-bilking aristocracy. The eighteenth century, as he sees it, is sticking out into the nineteenth in the person of the wicked Lord Steyne. *Vanity Fair* is a full-length version of what Dickens did for a few chapters in *Little Dorrit*. But by origins and upbringing Thackeray happens to be somewhat nearer to the class he is satirizing. Consequently he can produce such comparatively subtle types as, for instance, Major Pendennis and Rawdon Crawley. Major Pendennis is a shallow old snob, and Rawdon Crawley is a thick-headed ruffian who sees nothing wrong in living for years by swindling tradesmen; but what Thackery realizes is that according to their tortuous code they are neither of them bad men. Major Pendennis would not sign a dud cheque, for instance; Rawdon certainly would, but on the other hand he would not desert a friend in a tight corner. Both of them would behave well on the field of battle – a thing that would not particularly appeal to Dickens. The result is that at the end one is left with a kind of amused tolerance for Major Pendennis and with something approaching respect for Rawdon; and yet one sees, better than any diatribe could make one, the utter rottenness of that kind of cadging, toadying life on the fringes of smart society. Dickens would be quite incapable of this. In his hands both Rawdon and the Major would dwindle to traditional caricatures. And, on the whole, his attacks on 'good' society are rather perfunctory. The aristocracy and the big bourgeoisie exist in his books chiefly as a kind of 'noises off', a haw-hawing chorus somewhere in the wings, like Podsnap's dinner-parties. When he produces a really subtle and damaging portrait, like John Dorrit or Harold Skimpole, it is generally of some rather middling, unimportant person.

One very striking thing about Dickens, especially considering the time he lived in, is his lack of vulgar nationalism. All peoples who have reached the point of becoming nations tend to despise foreigners, but there is not much doubt that the English-speaking races are the worst offenders. One can see this from the fact that as soon as they become fully aware of any foreign race they invent an insulting nickname for it. Wop, Dago, Froggy, Squarehead, Kike, Sheeny, Nigger, Wog, Chink, Greaser, Yellowbelly – these are merely a selection. Any time before 1870 the list would have been shorter, because the map of the world was different from what it is now, and there were only three or four foreign races that had fully entered into the English consciousness. But towards these, and especially towards France, the nearest and best-hated nation, the English attitude of patronage was so intolerable that English 'arrogance' and 'xenophobia' are still a legend. And of course they are not a completely untrue legend even now. Till very recently nearly all English children were brought up to despise the southern European races, and history as taught in schools was mainly a list of battles won by England. But one has got to read, say, the *Quarterly Review* of the thirties to know what boasting really is. Those were the days when the English built up their legend of themselves as 'sturdy islanders' and 'stubborn hearts of oak' and when it was accepted as a kind of scientific fact that one Englishman was the equal of three foreigners. All through nineteenth-century novels and comic papers there runs the traditional figure of the 'Froggy' – a small ridiculous man with a tiny beard and a pointed top-hat, always jabbering and gesticulating, vain, frivolous and fond of boasting of his martial exploits, but generally taking to flight when real danger appears. Over against him was John Bull, the 'sturdy English yeoman', or (a more public-school version) the 'strong, silent Englishman' of Charles Kingsley, Tom Hughes and others.

Thackeray, for instance, has this outlook very strongly, though there are moments when he sees through it and laughs at it. The one historical fact that is firmly fixed in his mind is that the English won the battle of Waterloo. One never reads far in his books without coming upon some reference to it. The English, as he sees it, are invincible because of their tremendous physical strength, due mainly to living on beef. Like most Englishmen of his time, he has the curious illusion that the English are larger than other people (Thackeray, as it happened, *was* larger than most people), and therefore he is capable of writing passages like this :

I say to you that you are better than a Frenchman. I would lay even money that you who are reading this are more than five feet seven in height, and weigh eleven stone; while a Frenchman is five feet four and does not weigh nine. The Frenchman has after his soup a dish of vegetables, where you have one of meat. You are a different and superior animal – a French-beating animal (the history of hundreds of years has shown you to be so), etc. etc.

There are similar passages scattered all through Thackeray's works. Dickens would never be guilty of anything of that kind. It would be an exaggeration to say that he nowhere pokes fun at foreigners, and of course like nearly all nineteenth-century Englishmen, he is untouched by European culture. But never anywhere does he indulge in the typical English boasting, the 'island race', 'bulldog breed', 'right little, tight little island' style of talk. In the whole of *A Tale of Two Cities* there is not a line that could be taken as meaning, 'Look how these wicked Frenchmen behave!' The only place where he seems to display a normal hatred of foreigners is in the American chapters of *Martin Chuzzlewit*. This, however, is simply the reaction of a generous mind against cant. If Dickens were alive today he would make a trip to Soviet Russia and come back to the book rather like Gide's *Retour de L'URSS*. But he is remarkably free from the idiocy of regarding nations as individuals. He seldom even makes jokes turning on nationality. He does not exploit the comic Irishman and the comic Welshman, for instance, and not because he objects to stock characters and ready-made jokes, which obviously he does not. It is perhaps more significant that he shows no prejudice against Jews. It is true that he takes it for granted (*Oliver Twist* and *Great Expectations*) that a receiver of stolen goods will be a Jew, which at the time was probably justified. But the 'Jew joke', endemic in English literature until the rise of Hitler, does not appear in his books, and in *Our Mutual Friend* he makes a pious though not very convincing attempt to stand up for the Jews.

Dickens's lack of vulgar nationalism is in part the mark of a real largeness of mind, and in part results from his negative, rather unhelpful political attitude. He is very much an Englishman but he is hardly aware of it – certainly the thought of being an Englishman does not thrill him. He has no imperialist feelings, no discernible views on foreign politics, and is untouched by the military tradition. Temperamentally he is much nearer to the small noncomformist tradesman who looks down on the 'redcoats', and thinks that war is wicked – a one-eyed view, but after all, war *is* wicked. It is noticeable that Dickens hardly writes of war, even to denounce it. With all his marvellous powers of description, and of describing things he had never seen, he never describes a battle, unless one counts the attack on the Bastille in *A Tale of Two Cities*. Probably the subject would not strike him as interesting, and in any case he would not regard a battlefield as a place where anything worth settling could be settled. It is one up to the lower-middle-class, puritan mentality.

III

Dickens had grown up near enough to poverty to be terrified of it, and in spite of his generosity of mind, he is not free from the special prejudices of the shabby-genteel. It is usual to claim him as a 'popular' writer, a champion of the 'oppressed masses'. So he is, so long as he thinks of them as oppressed; but there are two things that condition his attitude. In the first place, he is a south-of-England man, and a Cockney at that, and therefore out of touch with the bulk of the real oppressed masses, the industrial and agricultural labourers. It is interesting to see how Chesterton, another Cockney, always presents Dickens as the spokesman of 'the poor', without showing much awareness of who 'the poor' really are. To Chesterton 'the poor' means small shopkeepers and servants. Sam Weller, he says, 'is the great symbol in English literature of the populace peculiar to England'; and Sam Weller is a valet! The other point is that Dickens's early experiences have given him a horror of proletarian roughness. He shows this unmistakably whenever he writes of the very poorest of the poor, the slum-dwellers. His descriptions of the London slums are always full of undisguised repulsion :

The ways were foul and narrow; the shops and houses wretched; and people half naked, drunken, slipshod and ugly. Alleys and archways, like so many cesspools, disgorged their offences of smell, and dirt, and life, upon the straggling streets; and the whole quarter reeked with crime, and filth, and misery, etc. etc.

There are many similar passages in Dickens. From them one gets the impression of whole submerged populations whom he regards as being beyond the pale. In rather the same way the modern doctrinaire Socialist contemptuously writes off a large block of the population as 'lumpenproletariat'. Dickens also shows less understanding of criminals than one would expect of him. Although he is well aware of the social and economic causes of crime, he often seems to feel that when a man has once broken the law he has put himself outside human society. There is a chapter at the end of *David Copperfield* in which David visits the prison where Latimer and Uriah Heep are serving their sentences. Dickens actually seems to regard the horrible 'model' prisons, against which Charles Reade delivered his memorable attack in *It is Never too Late to Mend*, as too humane. He complains that the food is too good! As soon as he comes up against crime or the worst depths of poverty, he shows traces of the 'I've always kept myself respectable' habit of mind. The attitude of Pip (obviously the attitude of Dickens himself) towards Magwitch in *Great Expectations* is extremely interesting. Pip is conscious all along of his ingratitude towards Joe, but far less so of his ingratitude towards Magwitch. When he discovers that the person who has loaded him with benefits for years is actually a transported convict, he falls into frenzies of disgust. 'The abhorrence in which I held the man, the dread I had of him, the repugnance with which I shrank from him, could not have been exceeded if he had been some terrible beast,' etc. etc. So far as one can discover from the text, this is not because when Pip was a child he had been terrorized by Magwitch in the churchyard; it is because Magwitch is a criminal and a convict. There is an even more 'kept-myself-respectable' touch in the fact that Pip feels as a matter of course that he cannot take Magwitch's money. The money is not the product of a crime, it has been honestly acquired; but it is an ex-convict's money and therefore 'tainted'. There is nothing psychologically false in this, either. Psychologically the latter part of *Great Expectations* is about the best thing Dickens ever did; throughout this part of the book one feels 'Yes, that is just how Pip would have behaved.' But the point is that in the matter of Magwitch, Dickens identifies with Pip, and his attitude is at bottom snobbish. The result is that Magwitch belongs to the same queer class of characters as Falstaff and, probably, Don Quixote – characters who are more pathetic than the author intended.

When it is a question of the non-criminal poor, the ordinary, decent, labouring poor, there is of course nothing contemptuous in Dickens's attitude. He has the sincerest admiration for people like the Peggottys and the Plornishes. But it is questionable whether he really regards them as equals. It is of the greatest interest to read Chapter XI of *David Copperfield* and side by side with it the autobiographical fragments (parts of this are given in Forster's *Life*), in which Dickens expresses his feelings about the blacking-factory episode a great deal more strongly than in the novel. For more than twenty years afterwards the memory was so painful to him that he would go out of his way to avoid that part of the Strand. He says that to pass that way 'made me cry, after my eldest child could speak'. The text makes it quite clear that what hurt him most of all, then and in retrospect, was the enforced contact with 'low' associates:

No words can express the secret agony of my soul as I sunk into this companionship; compared these everyday associates with those of my happier childhood. But I held some station at the blacking warehouse too ... I soon became at least as expeditious and as skilful with my hands as either of the other boys. Though perfectly familiar with them, my conduct and manners were different enough from theirs to place a space between us. They, and the men, always spoke of me as 'the young gentleman'. A certain man ... used to call me 'Charles' sometimes in speaking to me; but I think it was mostly when we were very confidential.... Poll Green uprose once, and rebelled against the 'young-gentleman' usage; but Bob Fagin settled him speedily.

It was as well that there should be 'a space between us', you see. However much Dickens may admire the working classes, he does not wish to resemble them. Given his origins, and the time he lived in, it could hardly be otherwise. In the early nineteenth century class animosities may have been no sharper than they are now, but the surface differences between class and class were enormously greater. The 'gentleman' and the 'common man' must have seemed like different species of animal. Dickens is quite genuinely on the side of the poor against the rich, but it would be next door to impossible for him not to think of a working-class exterior as a stigma. In one of Tolstoy's fables the peasants of a certain village judge every stranger who arrives from the state of his hands. If his palms are hard from work, they let him in; if his palms are soft, out he goes. This would be hardly intelligible to Dickens; all his heroes have soft hands. His younger heroes – Nicholas Nickleby, Martin Chuzzlewit, Edward Chester, David Copperfield, John Harmon – are usually of the type known as 'walking gentlemen'. He likes a bourgeois exterior and a bourgeois (not aristocratic) accent. One curious symptom of this is that he will not allow anyone who is to play a heroic part to speak like a working man. A comic hero like Sam Weller, or a merely pathetic figure like Stephen Blackpool, can speak with a broad accent, but the *jeune premier* always speaks the equivalent of B.B.C. This is so, even when it involves absurdities. Little Pip, for instance, is brought up by people speaking broad Essex, but talks upper-class English from his earliest childhood; actually he would have talked the same dialect as Joe, or at least as Mrs Gargery. So also with Biddy Wopsle, Lizzie Hexam, Sissie Jupe, Oliver Twist – one ought perhaps to add Little Dorrit. Even Rachel in *Hard Times* has barely a trace of Lancashire accent, an impossibility in her case.

One thing that often gives the clue to a novelist's real feelings on the class question is the attitude he takes up when class collides with sex. This is a thing too painful to be lied about, and consequently it is one of the points at which the 'I'm-not-a-snob' pose tends to break down.

One sees that at its most obvious where a class-distinction is also a colour-distinction. And something resembling the colonial attitude ('native' women are fair game, white women are sacrosanct) exists in a veiled form in all-white communities, causing bitter resentment on both sides. When this issue arises, novelists often revert to crude class-feelings which they might disclaim at other times. A good example of 'class-conscious' reaction is a rather forgotten novel, *The People of Clopton*, by Andrew Barton. The author's moral code is quite clearly mixed up with class-hatred. He feels the seduction of a poor girl by a rich man to be something atrocious, a kind of defilement, something quite different from her seduction by a man in her own walk of life. Trollope deals with this theme twice (*The Three Clerks* and *The Small House at Allington*) and, as one might expect, entirely from the upper-class angle. As he sees it, an affair with a barmaid or a landlady's daughter is simply an 'entanglement' to be escaped from. Trollope's moral standards are strict, and he does not allow the seduction actually to happen, but the implication is always that a working-class girl's feelings do not greatly matter. In *The Three Clerks* he even gives the typical class-reaction by noting that the girl 'smells'. Meredith (*Rhoda Fleming*) takes more the 'class-conscious' viewpoint. Thackeray, as often, seems to hesitate. In *Pendennis* (Fanny Bolton) his attitude is much the same as Trollope's; in *A Shabby Genteel Story* it is nearer to Meredith's.

One could divine a great deal about Trollope's social origin, or Meredith's, or Barton's, merely from their hand-ling of the class-sex theme. So one can with Dickens, but what emerges, as usual, is that he is more inclined to identify himself with the middle class than with the proletariat. The one incident that seems to contradict this is the tale of the young peasant-girl in Doctor Manette's manuscript in *A Tale of Two Cities*. This, however, is merely a costume-piece put in to explain the implacable hatred of Madame Defarge, which Dickens does not pretend to approve of. In *David Copperfield*, where he is dealing with a typical nine-teenth-century seduction, the class-issue does not seem to strike him as paramount. It is a law of Victorian novels that sexual misdeeds must not go unpunished, and so Steerforth is drowned on Yarmouth sands, but neither Dickens, nor old Peggotty, nor even Ham, seems to feel that Steerforth has added to his offence by being the son of rich parents. The Steerforths are moved by class-motives, but the Peg-gottys are not – not even in the scene between Mrs Steerforth and old Peggotty; if they were, of course, they would prob-ably turn against David as well as against Steerforth.

In *Our Mutual Friend* Dickens treats the episode of Eugene Wrayburn and Lizzie Hexam very realistically and with no appearance of class bias. According to the 'Unhand me, monster!' tradition, Lizzie ought either to 'spurn' Eugene or to be ruined by him and throw herself off Waterloo Bridge: Eugene ought to be either a heartless betrayer or a hero resolved upon defying society. Neither behaves in the least like this. Lizzie is frightened by Eugene's advances and actually runs away from him, but hardly pretends to dislike them; Eugene is attracted by her, has too much decency to attempt seducing her and dare not marry her because of his family. Finally they are married and no one is any the worse, except Mrs Twemlow, who will lose a few dinner engagements. It is all very much as it might have happened in real life. But a 'class-conscious' novelist would have given her to Bradley Headstone.

But when it is the other way about – when it is a case of a poor man aspiring to some woman who is 'above' him – Dickens instantly retreats into the middle-class attitude. He is rather fond of the Victorian notion of a woman (woman with a capital W) being 'above' a man. Pip feels that Estella is 'above' him, Esther Summerson is 'above' Guppy, Little Dorrit is 'above' John Chivery, Lucy Manette is 'above' Sydney Carton. In some of these the 'above'-ness is merely moral, but in others it is social. There is a scarcely mistakable class-reaction when David Copperfield discovers that Uriah Heep is plotting to marry Agnes Wickfield. The disgusting Uriah suddenly announces that he is in love with her:

'Oh, Master Copperfield, with what a pure affection do I love the ground my Agnes walks on.'
I believe I had the delirious idea of seizing the red-hot poker out of the fire, and running him through with it. It went from me with a shock, like a ball fired from a rifle: but the image of Agnes, outraged by so much as a thought of this red-headed animal's, remained in my mind (when I looked at him, sitting all awry as if his mean soul griped his body) and made me giddy. ... 'I believe Agnes Wickfield to be as far above *you* [David

says later on], and as far removed from all *your* aspirations, as the moon herself.'

Considering how Heep's general lowness – his servile manners, dropped aitches and so forth – has been rubbed in throughout the book, there is not much doubt about the nature of Dickens's feelings. Heep, of course, is playing a villainous part, but even villains have sexual lives; it is the thought of the 'pure' Agnes in bed with a man who drops his aitches that really revolts Dickens. But his usual tendency is to treat a man in love with a woman who is 'above' him as a joke. It is one of the stock jokes of English literature, from Malvolio onwards. Guppy in *Bleak House* is an example, John Chivery is another, and there is a rather ill-natured treatment of this theme in the 'swarry' in *Pickwick Papers*. Here Dickens describes the Bath footmen as living a kind of fantasy-life, holding dinner-parties in imitation of their 'betters' and deluding themselves that their young mistresses are in love with them. This evidently strikes him as very comic. So it is in a way, though one might question whether it is not better for a footman even to have delusions of this kind than simply to accept his status in the spirit of the catechism.

In his attitude towards servants Dickens is not ahead of his age. In the nineteenth century the revolt against domestic service was just beginning, to the great annoyance of everyone with over £500 a year. An enormous number of the jokes in nineteenth-century comic papers deals with the uppishness of servants. For years *Punch* ran a series of jokes called 'Servant Gal-isms', all turning on the then astonishing fact that a servant is a human being. Dickens is sometimes guilty of this kind of thing himself. His books abound with the ordinary comic servants; they are dishonest (*Great Expectations*), incompetent (*David Copperfield*), turn up their noses at good food (*Pickwick Papers*), etc. etc. – all rather in the spirit of the suburban housewife with one downtrodden cook-general. But what is curious, in a nine-teenth-century radical, is that when he wants to draw a sympathetic picture of a servant, he creates what is recognizably a feudal type. Sam Weller, Mark Tapley, Clara Peggotty are all of them feudal figures. They belong to the *genre* of the 'old family retainer'; they identify themselves with their master's family and are at once doggishly faithful and completely familiar. No doubt Mark Tapley and Sam Weller are derived to some extent from Smollett, and hence from Cervantes; but it is interesting that Dickens should have been attracted by such a type. Sam Weller's attitude is definitely medieval. He gets himself arrested in order to follow Mr Pickwick into the Fleet, and afterwards refuses to get married because he feels that Mr Pickwick still needs his services. There is a characteristic scene between them:

'Vages or no vages, board or no board, lodgin' or no lodgin', Sam Veller, as you took from the old inn in the Borough, sticks by you, come what may...'

'My good fellow,' said Mr Pickwick, when Mr Weller had sat down again, rather abashed at his own enthusiasm, 'you are bound to consider the young woman also.'

'I do consider the young 'ooman, sir,' said Sam. 'I have considered the young 'ooman. I've spoke to her. I've told her how I'm sitivated; she's ready to vait till I'm ready, and I believe she vill. If she don't, she's not the young 'ooman I take her for, and I give up with readiness.'

It is easy to imagine what the young woman would have said to this in real life. But notice the feudal atmosphere. Sam Weller is ready as a matter of course to sacrifice years of his life to his master, and he can also sit down in his master's presence. A modern manservant would never think of doing either. Dickens's views on the servant question do not get much beyond wishing that master and servant would love one another. Sloppy in *Our Mutual Friend*, though a wretched failure as a character, represents the same kind of loyalty as Sam Weller. Such loyalty, of course, is natural, human, and likeable; but so was feudalism.

What Dickens seems to be doing, as usual, is to reach out for an idealized version of the existing thing. He was writing at a time when domestic service must have seemed a completely inevitable evil. There were no labour-saving devices, and there was huge inequality of wealth. It was an age of enormous families, pretentious meals and inconvenient houses, when the slavey drudging fourteen hours a day in the basement kitchen was something too normal to be noticed. And given the *fact* of servitude, the feudal relationship is the only tolerable one. Sam Weller and Mark Tapley are dream figures, no less than the Cheerybles. If there have got to be masters and servants, how much better that the master should be Mr Pickwick and the servant should be Sam Weller. Better still, of course, if servants did not exist at all – but this Dickens is probably unable to imagine. Without a high level of mechanical development, human equality is not practically possible; Dickens goes to show that it is not imaginable either.

IV

It is not merely a coincidence that Dickens never writes about agriculture and writes endlessly about food. He was a Cockney, and London is the centre of the earth in rather the same sense that the belly is the centre of the body. It is a city of consumers, of people who are deeply civilized but not primarily useful. A thing that strikes one when one looks below the surface of Dickens's books is that, as nineteenth-century novelists go, he is rather ignorant. He knows very little about the way things really happen. At first sight this statement looks flatly untrue and it needs some qualification.

Dickens had had vivid glimpses of 'low life' – life in a debtor's prison, for example – and he was also a popular novelist and able to write about ordinary people. So were all the characteristic English novelists of the nineteenth century. They felt at home in the world they lived in, whereas a writer nowadays is so hopelessly isolated that the typical modern novel is a novel about a novelist. Even when Joyce, for instance, spends a decade or so in patient efforts to make contact with the 'common man', his 'common man' finally turns out to be a Jew, and a bit of a highbrow at that. Dickens at least does not suffer from this kind of thing. He has no difficulty in introducing the common motives, love, ambition, avarice, vengeance and so forth. What he does not noticeably write about, however, is *work*.

In Dickens's novels anything in the nature of work happens off-stage. The only one of his heroes who has a plausible profession is David Copperfield, who is first a shorthand writer and then a novelist, like Dickens himself. With most of the others, the way they earn their living is very much in the background. Pip, for instance, 'goes into business' in Egypt; we are not told what business, and Pip's working life occupies about half a page of the book. Clennam has been in some unspecified business in China, and later goes into another barely specified business with Doyce; Martin Chuzzlewit is an architect, but does not seem to get much time for practising. In no case do their adventures spring directly out of their work. Here the contrast between Dickens and, say, Trollope is startling. And one reason for this is undoubtedly that Dickens knows very little about the professions his characters are supposed to follow. What exactly went on in Gradgrind's factories? How did Podsnap make his money? How did Merdle work his swindles? One knows that Dickens could never follow up the details of Parliamentary elections and Stock Exchange rackets as Trollope could. As soon as he has to deal with trade, finance, industry or politics he takes refuge in vagueness, or in satire. This is the case even with legal processes, about which actually he must have known a good deal. Compare any lawsuit in Dickens with the lawsuit in *Orley Farm*, for instance.

And this partly accounts for the needless ramifications of Dickens's novels, the awful Victorian 'plot'. It is true that not all his novels are alike in this. *A Tale of Two Cities* is a very good and fairly simple story, and so in its different ways is *Hard Times*; but these are just the two which are always rejected as 'not like Dickens' – and incidentally they were not published in monthly numbers.* The two first-person novels are also good stories, apart from their sub-plots. But the typical Dickens novel, *Nicholas Nickleby, Oliver Twist, Martin Chuzzlewit, Our Mutual Friend*, always exists round a framework of melodrama. The last thing anyone ever remembers about the books is their central story. On the other hand, I suppose no one has ever read them without carrying the memory of individual pages to the day of his death. Dickens sees human beings with the most intense vividness, but sees them always in private life, as 'characters', not as functional members of society; that is to say, he sees them statically. Consequently his greatest success is *The Pickwick Papers*, which is not a story at all, merely a series of sketches; there is little attempt at development – the characters simply go on and on, behaving like

* *Hard Times* was published as a serial in *Household Words* and *Great Expectations* and *A Tale of Two Cities* in *All the Year Round*. Forster says that the shortness of the weekly instalments made it 'much more difficult to get sufficient interest into each'. Dickens himself complained of the lack of 'elbow-room'. In other words, he had to stick more closely to the story.

idiots, in a kind of eternity. As soon as he tries to bring his characters into action, the melodrama begins. He cannot make the action revolve round their ordinary occupations; hence the crossword puzzle of coincidences, intrigues, murders, disguises, buried wills, long-lost brothers, etc. etc. In the end even people like Squeers and Micawber get sucked into the machinery.

Of course it would be absurd to say that Dickens is a vague or merely melodramatic writer. Much that he wrote is extremely factual, and in the power of evoking visual images he has probably never been equalled. When Dickens has once described something you see it for the rest of your life. But in a way the concreteness of his vision is a sign of what he is missing. For, after all, that is what the merely casual onlooker always sees – the outward appearance, the non-functional, the surfaces of things. No one who is really involved in the landscape ever sees the landscape. Wonderfully as he can describe an *appearance*, Dickens does not often describe a *process*. The vivid pictures that he succeeds in leaving in one's memory are nearly always the pictures of things seen in leisure moments, in the coffee-rooms of country inns or through the windows of a stage-coach; the kind of things he notices are inn-signs, brass door-knockers, painted jugs, the interiors of shops and private houses, clothes, faces and, above all, food. Everything is seen from the consumer-angle. When he writes about Cokestown he manages to evoke, in just a few paragraphs, the atmosphere of a Lancashire town as a slightly disgusted southern visitor would see it. 'It had a black canal in it, and a river that ran purple with evil-smelling dye, and vast piles of buildings full of windows where there was a rattling and a trembling all day long, where the piston of the steam-engine worked monotonously up and down, like the head of an elephant in a state of melancholy madness.'

That is as near as Dickens ever gets to the machinery of the mills. An engineer or a cotton-broker would see it differently; but then neither of them would be capable of that impressionistic touch about the heads of the elephants.

In a rather different sense his attitude to life is extremely unphysical. He is a man who lives through his eyes and ears rather than through his hands and muscles. Actually his habits were not so sedentary as this seems to imply. In spite of rather poor health and physique, he was active to the point of restlessness; throughout his life he was a remarkable walker, and he could at any rate carpenter well enough to put up stage scenery. But he was not one of those people who feel a need to use their hands. It is difficult to imagine him digging at a cabbage-patch, for instance. He gives no evidence of knowing anything about agriculture, and obviously knows nothing about any kind of game or sport. He has no interest in pugilism, for instance. Considering the age in which he was writing, it is astonishing how little physical brutality there is in Dickens's novels. Martin Chuzzlewit and Mark Tapley, for instance, behave with the most remarkable mildness towards the Americans who are constantly menacing them with revolvers and bowie-knives. The average English or American novelist would have had them handing out socks on the jaw and exchanging pistol-shots in all directions. Dickens is too decent for that; he sees the stupidity of violence, and he also belongs to a cautious urban class which does not deal in socks on the jaw, even in theory. And his attitude towards sport is mixed up with social feelings. In England, for mainly geographical reasons, sport, especially field-sports, and snobbery are inextricably mingled. English Socialists are often flatly incredulous when told that Lenin, for instance, was devoted to shooting. In their eyes, shooting, hunting, etc., are simply snobbish observances of the landed gentry; they forget that these things might appear differently in a huge virgin country like Russia. From Dickens's point of view almost any kind of sport is at best a subject for satire. Consequently one side of nineteenth-century life – the boxing, racing, cock-fighting, badger-digging, poaching, rat-catching side of life, so wonderfully embalmed in Leech's illustrations to Surtees – is outside his scope.

What is more striking, in a seemingly 'progressive' radical, is that he is not mechanically minded. He shows no interest either in the details of machinery or in the things machinery can do. As Gissing remarks, Dickens nowhere describes a railway journey with anything like the enthusiasm he shows in describing journeys by stage-coach. In nearly all of his books one has a curious feeling that one is living in the first quarter of the nineteenth century, and in fact, he does tend to return to this period. *Little Dorrit*, written in the middle fifties, deals with the late twenties; *Great Expectations* (1861) is not dated, but evidently deals with the twenties and thirties. Several of the inventions and discoveries which have made the modern world possible (the electric telegraph, the breech-loading gun, india-rubber, coal gas, wood-pulp paper) first appeared in Dickens's lifetime, but he scarcely notes them in his books. Nothing is queerer than the vagueness with which he speaks of Doyce's 'invention' in *Little Dorrit*. It is represented as something extremely ingenious and revolutionary, 'of great importance to his country and his fellow-creatures', and it is also an important minor link in the book; yet we are never told what the 'invention' is! On the other hand, Doyce's physical appearance is hit off with the typical Dickens touch; he has a peculiar way of moving his thumb, a way characteristic of engineers. After that, Doyce is firmly anchored in one's memory; but, as usual, Dickens has done it by fastening on something external.

There are people (Tennyson is an example) who lack the mechanical faculty but can see the social possibilities of machinery. Dickens has not this stamp of mind. He shows very little consciousness of the future. When he speaks of human progress it is usually in terms of *moral* progress – men growing better; probably he would never admit that men are only as good as their technical development allows them to be. At this point the gap between Dickens and his modern analogue, H. G. Wells, is at its widest. Wells wears the future round his neck like a mill-stone, but Dickens's unscientific cast of mind is just as damaging in a different way. What it does is to make any *positive* attitude more difficult for him. He is hostile to the feudal, agricultural past and not in real touch with the industrial present. Well, then, all that remains is the future (meaning Science, 'progress', and so forth), which hardly enters into his thoughts. Therefore, while attacking everything in sight, he has no definable standard of comparison. As I have pointed out already, he attacks the current educational system with perfect justice, and yet, after all, he has no remedy to offer except kindlier schoolmasters. Why did he not indicate what a school *might* have been? Why did he not have his own sons educated according to some plan of his own, instead of sending them to public schools to be stuffed with Greek? Because he lacked that kind of imagination. He has an infallible moral sense, but very little intellectual curiosity. And here one comes upon something which really is an enormous deficiency in Dickens, something that really does make the nineteenth century seem remote from us – that he has no idea of *work*.

With the doubtful exception of David Copperfield (merely Dickens himself), one cannot point to a single one of his central characters who is primarily interested in his job. His heroes work in order to make a living and to marry the heroine, not because they feel a passionate interest in one particular subject. Martin Chuzzlewit, for instance, is not burning with zeal to be an architect; he might just as well be a doctor or a barrister. In any case, in the typical Dickens novel, the *deus ex machina* enters with a bag of gold in the last chapter and the hero is absolved from further struggle. The feeling 'This is what I came into the world to do. Everything else is uninteresting. I will do this even if it means starvation', which turns men of differing temperaments into scientists, inventors, artists, priests, explorers and revolutionaries – this motif is almost entirely absent from Dickens's books. He himself, as is well known, worked like a slave and believed in his work as few novelists have ever done. But there seems to be no calling except novel-writing (and perhaps acting) towards which he can imagine this kind of devotion. And, after all, it is natural enough, considering his rather negative attitude towards society. In the last resort there is nothing he admires except common decency. Science is uninteresting and machinery is cruel and ugly (the heads of the elephants). Business is only for ruffians like Bounderby. As for politics – leave that to the Tite Barnacles. Really there is no objective except to marry the heroine, settle down, live solvently and be kind. And you can do that much better in private life.

Here, perhaps, one gets a glimpse of Dickens's secret imaginative background. What did he think of as the most desirable way to live? When Martin Chuzzlewit had made it up with his uncle, when Nicholas Nickleby had married money, when John Harman had been enriched by Boffin – what did they *do*?

The answer evidently is that they did nothing. Nicholas Nickleby invested his wife's money with the Cheerybles and 'became a rich and prosperous merchant', but as he immediately retired into Devonshire, we can assume that he did not work very hard. Mr and Mrs Snodgrass 'purchased and cultivated a small farm, more for occupation than profit'. That is the spirit in which most of Dickens's books end – a sort of radiant idleness. Where he appears to disapprove of young men who do not work (Harthouse, Harry Gowan, Richard Carstone, Wrayburn before his reformation) it is because they are cynical and immoral or because they are a burden on somebody else; if you are 'good', and also self-supporting, there is no reason why you should not spend fifty years in simply drawing your dividends. Home life is always enough. And, after all, it was the general assumption of his age. The 'genteel sufficiency', the 'competence', the 'gentleman of independent means' (or 'in easy circumstances') – the very phrases tell one all about the strange, empty dream of the eighteenth- and nineteenth-century middle bourgeoisie. It was a dream of *complete idleness*. Charles Reade conveys its spirit perfectly in the ending of *Hard Cash*. Alfred Hardie, hero of *Hard Cash*, is the typical nineteenth-century novel-hero (public-school style), with gifts which Reade describes as amounting to 'genius'. He is an old Etonian and a scholar of Oxford, he knows most of the Greek and Latin classics by heart, he can box with prize-fighters and win the Diamond Sculls at Henley. He goes through incredible adventures in which, of course, he be-haves with faultless heroism, and then, at the age of twenty-five, he inherits a fortune, marries his Julia Dodd and settles down in the suburbs of Liverpool, in the same house as his parents-in-law:

They all lived together at Albion Villa, thanks to Alfred. ... Oh, you happy little villa! You were as like Paradise as any mortal dwelling can be. A day came, however, when your walls could no longer hold all the happy inmates. Julia presented Alfred with a lovely boy; enter two nurses and the villa showed symptoms of bursting. Two months more, and Alfred and his wife overflowed into the next villa. It was but twenty yards off; and there was a double reason for the migration. As often happens after a long separation, Heaven bestowed on Captain and Mrs Dodd another infant to play about their knees, etc. etc. etc.

This is the type of the Victorian happy ending – a vision of a huge, loving family of three or four generations, all crammed together in the same house and constantly multiplying, like a bed of oysters. What is striking about it is the utterly soft, sheltered, effortless life that it implies. It is not even a violent idleness, like Squire Western's. That is the significance of Dickens's urban background and his non-interest in the blackguardly-sporting military side of life. His heroes, once they had come into money and 'settled down', would not only do no work; they would not even ride, hunt, shoot, fight duels, elope with actresses or lose money at the races. They would simply live at home in feather-bed respectability, and preferably next door to a blood-relation living exactly the same life:

The first act of Nicholas, when he became a rich and prosperous merchant, was to buy his father's old house. As time crept on, and there came gradually about him a group of lovely children, it was altered and enlarged; but none of the old rooms were ever pulled down, no old tree was ever rooted up, nothing with which there was any association of bygone times was ever removed or changed.

Within a stone's-throw was another retreat enlivened by children's pleasant voices too; and here was Kate ... the same true, gentle creature, the same fond sister, the same in the love of all about her, as in her girlish days.

It is the same incestuous atmosphere as in the passage quoted from Reade. And evidently this is Dickens's ideal ending. It is perfectly attained in *Nicholas Nickleby*, *Martin Chuzzlewit* and *Pickwick*, and it is approximated to in varying degrees in almost all the others. The exceptions are *Hard Times* and *Great Expectations* – the latter actually has a 'happy ending', but it contradicts the general tendency of the book, and it was put in at the request of Bulwer Lytton.

The ideal to be striven after, then, appears to be something like this: a hundred thousand pounds, a quaint old house with plenty of ivy on it, a sweetly womanly wife, a horde of children, and no work. Everything is safe, soft, peaceful and, above all, domestic. In the moss-grown churchyard down the road are the graves of the loved ones who passed away before the happy ending happened. The servants are comic and feudal, the children prattle round your feet, the old friends sit at your fireside, talking of past days, there is the endless succession of enormous meals, the cold punch and sherry negus, the feather beds and warming-pans, the Christmas parties with charades and blind man's buff; but nothing ever happens, except the yearly childbirth. The curious thing is that it is a genuinely happy picture, or so Dickens is able to make it appear. The thought of that kind of existence is satisfying to him. This alone would be enough to tell one that more than a hundred years have passed since Dickens's first book was written. No modern man could combine such purposelessness with so much vitality.

v

By this time anyone who is a lover of Dickens, and who has read as far as this, will probably be angry with me.

I have been discussing Dickens simply in terms of his 'message', and almost ignoring his literary qualities. But every writer, especially every novelist, *has* a 'message', whether he admits it or not, and the minutest details of his work are influenced by it. All art is propaganda. Neither Dickens himself nor the majority of Victorian novelists would have thought of denying this. On the other hand, not all propaganda is art. As I said earlier, Dickens is one of those writers who are felt to be worth stealing. He has been stolen by Marxists, by Catholics and, above all, by Conservatives. The question is, What is there to steal? Why does anyone care about Dickens? Why do I care about Dickens?

That kind of question is never easy to answer. As a rule, an aesthetic preference is either something inexplicable or it is so corrupted by non-aesthetic motives as to make one wonder whether the whole of literary criticism is not a huge network of humbug. In Dickens's case the complicating factor is his familiarity. He happens to be one of those 'great authors' who are ladled down everyone's throat in childhood. At the time this causes rebellion and vomiting, but it may have different after-effects in later life. For instance, nearly everyone feels a sneaking affection for the patriotic poems that he learned by heart as a child, 'Ye Mariners of England', the 'Charge of the Light Brigade' and so forth. What one enjoys is not so much the poems themselves as the memories they call up. And with Dickens the same forces of association are at work. Probably there are copies of one or two of his books lying about in an actual majority of English homes. Many children begin to know his characters by sight before they can even read, for on the whole Dickens was lucky in his illustrators. A thing that is absorbed as early as that does not come up against any critical judgement. And when one thinks of this, one thinks of all that is bad and silly in Dickens – the cast-iron 'plots', the characters who don't come off, the *longueurs,* the paragraphs in blank verse, the awful pages of 'pathos'. And then the thought arises, when I say I like Dickens, do I simply mean that I like thinking about my childhood? Is Dickens merely an institution?

If so, he is an institution that there is no getting away from. How often one really thinks about any writer, even a writer one cares for, is a difficult thing to decide; but I should doubt whether anyone who has actually read Dickens can go a week without remembering him in one context or another. Whether you approve of him or not, he is *there*, like the Nelson Column. At any moment some scene or character, which may come from some book you cannot even remember the name of, is liable to drop into your mind. Micawber's letters! Winkle in the witness-box! Mrs Gamp! Mrs Wititterly and Sir Tumley Snuffim! Todgers's! (George Gissing said that when he passed the Monument it was never of the Fire of London that he thought, always of Todgers's.) Mrs Leo Hunter! Squeers! Silas Wegg and the Decline and Fall-off of the Russian Empire! Miss Mills and the Desert of Sahara! Wopsle acting Hamlet! Mrs Jellyby! Mantalini, Jerry Cruncher, Barkis, Pumblechook, Tracy Tupman, Skimpole, Joe Gargery, Pecksniff – and so it goes on and on. It is not so much a series of books, it is more like a world. And not a purely comic world either, for part of what one remembers in Dickens is his Victorian morbidness and necrophilia and the blood-and-thunder scenes – the death of Sykes, Krook's spontaneous combustion, Fagin in the condemned cell, the women knitting round the guillotine. To a surprising extent all this has entered even into the minds of people who do not care about it. A music-hall comedian can (or at any rate could quite recently) go on the stage and impersonate Micawber or Mrs Gamp with a fair certainty of being understood, although not one in twenty of the audience had ever read a book of Dickens's right through. Even people who affect to despise him quote him unconsciously.

Dickens is a writer who can be imitated, up to a certain point. In genuinely popular literature – for instance, the Elephant and Castle version of *Sweeny Todd* – he has been plagiarized quite shamelessly. What has been imitated, however, is simply a tradition that Dickens himself took from earlier novelists and developed, the cult of 'character', i.e. eccentricity. The thing that cannot be imitated is his fertility of invention, which is invention not so much of characters, still less of 'situations', as of turns of phrase and concrete details. The outstanding, unmistakable mark of Dickens's writing is the *unnecessary detail*. Here is an example of what I mean. The story given below is not particularly funny, but there is one phrase in it that is as individual as a fingerprint. Mr Jack Hopkins, at Bob Sawyer's party, is telling the story of the child who swallowed its sister's necklace:

Next day, child swallowed two beads; the day after that, he treated himself to three, and so on, till in a week's time he had got through the necklace – five-and-twenty beads in all. The sister, who was an industrious girl and seldom treated herself to a bit of finery, cried her eyes out at the loss of the necklace; looked high and low for it; but I needn't say, didn't find it. A few days afterwards, the family were at dinner – baked shoulder of mutton and potatoes under it – the child, who wasn't hungry, was playing about the room, when suddenly there was the devil of a noise, like a small hailstorm. 'Don't do that, my boy,' says the father. 'I ain't a-doin' nothing,' said the child. 'Well, don't do it again,' said the father. There was a short silence, and then the noise began again, worse than ever. 'If you don't mind what I say, my boy,' said the father, 'you'll find yourself in bed, in something less than a pig's whisper.' He gave the child a shake to make him obedient, and such a rattling ensued as nobody ever heard before. 'Why dam' me, it's *in* the child,' said the father; 'he's got the croup in the wrong place!' 'No, I haven't, father,' said the child, beginning to cry, 'it's the necklace; I swallowed it, father.' The father caught the child up, and ran with him to the hospital, the beads in the boy's stomach rattling all the way with the jolting; and the people looking up in the air, and down in the cellars, to see where the unusual sound came from. 'He's in the hospital now,' said Jack Hopkins, 'and he makes such a devil of a noise when he walks about, that they're obliged to muffle him in a watchman's coat, for fear he should wake the patients.'

As a whole, this story might come out of any nineteenth-century comic paper. But the unmistakable Dickens touch, the thing that nobody else would have thought of, is the baked shoulder of mutton and potatoes under it. How does this advance the story? The answer is that it doesn't. It is something totally unnecessary, a florid little squiggle on the edge of the page; only, it is by just these squiggles that the special Dickens atmosphere is created. The other thing one would notice here is that Dickens's way of telling a story takes a long time. An interesting example, too long to quote, is Sam Weller's story of the obstinate patient in Chapter XLIV of *The Pickwick Papers*. As it happens, we have a standard of comparison here, because Dickens is plagiarizing, consciously or unconsciously. The story is also told by some ancient Greek writer. I cannot now find the passage, but I read it years ago as a boy at school, and it runs more or less like this:

A certain Thracian, renowned for his obstinacy, was warned by his physician that if he drank a flagon of wine it would kill him. The Thracian thereupon drank the flagon of wine and immediately jumped off the house-top and perished. 'For,' said he, 'in this way I shall prove that the wine did not kill me.'

As the Greek tells it, that is the whole story – about six lines. As Sam Weller tells it, it takes round about a thousand words. Long before getting to the point we have been told all about the patient's clothes, his meals, his manners, even the newspapers he reads, and about the peculiar construction of the doctor's carriage, which conceals the fact that the coachman's trousers do not match his coat. Then there is the dialogue between the doctor and the patient. ' "Crumpets is wholesome, sir," said the patient. "Crumpets is *not* wholesome, sir," says the doctor, wery fierce," ' etc., etc. In the end the original story had been buried under the details. And in all of Dickens's most characteristic passages it is the same. His imagination overwhelms everything, like a kind of weed. Squeers stands up to address his boys, and immediately we are hearing about Bolder's father who was two pounds ten short, and Mobbs's stepmother who took to her bed on hearing that Mobbs wouldn't eat fat and hoped Mr Squeers would flog him into a happier state of mind. Mrs Leo Hunter writes a poem, 'Expiring Frog'; two full stanzas are given. Boffin takes a fancy to pose as a miser, and instantly we are down among the squalid biographies of eighteenth-century misers, with names like Vulture Hopkins and the Rev. Blewberry Jones, and chapter headings like 'The Story of the Mutton Pies' and 'The Treasures of a Dunghill'. Mrs Harris, who does not even exist, has more detail piled on to her than any three characters in an ordinary novel. Merely in the middle of a sentence we learn, for instance, that her infant nephew has been seen in a bottle at Greenwich Fair, along with the pink-eyed lady, the Prussian dwarf and the living skeleton. Joe Gargery describes how the robbers broke into the house of Pumblechook, the corn and seed merchant – 'and they took his till, and they took his cashbox, and they drinked his wine, and they partook of his wittles, and they slapped his face, and they pulled his nose, and they tied him up to his bedpust, and they give him a dozen, and they stuffed his mouth full of flowering annuals to perwent his crying out.' Once again the unmistakable Dickens touch, the flowering annuals; but any other novelist would only have mentioned about half of these outrages. Everything is piled up and up, detail on detail, embroidery on embroidery. It is futile to object that this kind of thing is rococo – one might as well make the same objection to a wedding-cake. Either you like it or you do not like it. Other nineteenth-century writers, Surtees, Barham, Thackeray, even Marryat, have something of Dickens's profuse, overflowing quality, but none of them on anything like the same scale. The appeal of all these writers now depends partly on period-flavour and though Marryat is still officially a 'boy's writer' and Surtees has a sort of legendary fame among hunting men, it is probable that they are read mostly by bookish people.

Significantly, Dickens's most successful books (not his *best* books) are *The Pickwick Papers*, which is not a novel, and *Hard Times* and *A Tale of Two Cities*, which are not funny. As a novelist his natural fertility greatly hampers him, because the burlesque which he is never able to resist, is constantly breaking into what ought to be serious situations. There is a good example of this in the opening chapter of *Great Expectations*. The escaped convict, Magwitch, has just captured the six-year-old Pip in the churchyard. The scene starts terrifyingly enough, from Pip's point of view. The convict, smothered in mud and with his chain trailing from his leg, suddenly starts up among the tombs, grabs the child, turns him upside down and robs his pockets. Then he begins terrorizing him into bringing food and a file:

He held me by the arms in an upright position on the top of the stone, and went on in these fearful terms:

'You bring me, tomorrow morning early, that file and them wittles. You bring the lot to me, at that old Battery over yonder. You do it and you never dare to say a word or dare to make a sign concerning your having seen such a person as me, or any person sumever, and you shall be let to live. You fail, or you go from my words in any partickler, no matter how small it is, and your heart and liver shall be tore out, roasted and ate. Now, I ain't alone, as you may think I am. There's a young man hid with me, in comparison with which young man I am a Angel.

That young man hears the words I speak. That young man has a secret way pecooliar to himself, of getting at a boy, and at his heart, and at his liver. It is in wain for a boy to attempt to hide himself from that young man. A boy may lock his doors, may be warm in bed, may tuck himself up, may draw the clothes over his head, may think himself comfortable and safe, but that young man will softly creep his way to him and tear him open. I am keeping that young man from harming you at the present moment, but with great difficulty. I find it wery hard to hold that young man off of your inside. Now, what do you say?'

Here Dickens has simply yielded to temptation. To begin with, no starving and hunted man would speak in the least like that. Moreover, although the speech shows a remarkable knowledge of the way in which a child's mind works, its actual words are quite out of tune with what is to follow. It turns Magwitch into a sort of pantomime wicked uncle, or, if one sees him through the child's eyes, into an appalling monster. Later in the book he is to be represented as neither, and his exaggerated gratitude, on which the plot turns, is to be incredible because of just this speech. As usual, Dickens's imagination has overwhelmed him. The picturesque details were too good to be left out. Even with characters who are more of a piece than Magwitch he is liable to be tripped up by some seductive phrase. Mr Murdstone, for instance, is in the habit of ending David Copperfield's lessons every morning with a dreadful sum in arithmetic. 'If I go into a cheesemonger's shop, and buy four thousand double-Gloucester cheeses at fourpence halfpenny each, present payment,' it always begins. Once again the typical Dickens detail, the double-Gloucester cheeses. But it is far too human a touch for Murdstone; he would have made it five thousand cashboxes. Every time this note is struck, the unity of the novel suffers. Not that it matters very much, because Dickens is obviously a writer whose parts are greater than his wholes.

He is all fragments, all details – rotten architecture, but wonderful gargoyles – and never better than when he is building up some character who will later on be forced to act inconsistently.

Of course it is not usual to urge against Dickens that he makes his characters behave inconsistently. Generally he is accused of doing just the opposite. His characters are supposed to be mere 'types', each crudely representing some single trait and fitted with a kind of label by which you recognize him. Dickens is 'only a caricaturist' – that is the usual accusation, and it does him both more and less than justice. To begin with, he did not think of himself as a caricaturist, and was constantly setting into action characters who ought to have been purely static. Squeers, Micawber, Miss Mowcher,* Wegg, Skimpole, Pecksniff and many others are finally involved in 'plots' where they are out of place and where they behave quite incredibly. They start off as magic-lantern slides and they end by getting mixed up in a third-rate movie. Sometimes one can put one's finger on a single sentence in which the original illusion is destroyed. There is such a sentence in *David Copperfield*. After the famous dinner-party (the one where the leg of mutton was underdone), David is showing his guests out. He stops Traddles at the top of the stairs :

'Traddles,' said I, 'Mr Micawber don't mean any harm, poor fellow : but if I were you I wouldn't lend him anything.'

'My dear Copperfield,' returned Traddles, smiling, 'I haven't got anything to lend.'

'You have got a name, you know,' I said.

At the place where one reads it this remark jars a little

*Dickens turned Miss Mowcher into a sort of heroine because the real woman whom he had caricatured had read the earlier chapters and was bitterly hurt. He had previously meant her to play a villainous part. But *any* action by such a character would seem incongruous.

though something of the kind was inevitable sooner or later. The story is a fairly realistic one, and David is growing up; ultimately he is bound to see Mr Micawber for what he is, a cadging scoundrel. Afterwards, of course, Dickens's sentimentality overcomes him and Micawber is made to turn over a new leaf. But from then on, the original Micawber is never quite recaptured, in spite of desperate efforts. As a rule, the 'plot' in which Dickens's characters get entangled is not particularly credible, but at least it makes some pretence at reality, whereas the world to which they belong is a never-never land, a kind of eternity. But just here one sees that 'only a caricaturist' is not really a condemnation. The fact that Dickens is always thought of as a caricaturist, although he was constantly trying to be something else, is perhaps the surest mark of his genius. The monstrosities that he created are still remembered as monstrosities, in spite of getting mixed up in would-be probable melodramas. Their first impact is so vivid that nothing that comes afterwards effaces it. As with the people one knew in childhood, one seems always to remember them in one particular attitude, doing one particular thing. Mrs Squeers is always ladling out brimstone and treacle, Mrs Gummidge is always weeping, Mrs. Gargery is always banging her husband's head against the wall, Mrs Jellyby is always scribbling tracts while her children fall into the area – and there they all are, fixed up for ever like little twinkling miniatures painted on snuffbox lids, completely fantastic and incredible, and yet somehow more solid and infinitely more memorable than the efforts of serious novelists. Even by the standards of his time Dickens was an exceptionally artificial writer. As Ruskin said, he 'chose to work in a circle of stage fire'. His characters are even more distorted and simplified than Smollett's. But there are no rules in novel-writing, and for any work of art there is only one test worth bothering about – survival. By this test Dickens's characters have succeeded, even if the people who remember them hardly think of them as human beings. They are monsters, but at any rate they *exist*.

But all the same there is a disadvantage in writing about monsters. It amounts to this, that it is only certain moods that Dickens can speak to. There are large areas of the human mind that he never touches. There is no poetic feeling anywhere in his books, and no genuine tragedy, and even sexual love is almost outside his scope. Actually his books are not so sexless as they are sometimes declared to be, and considering the time in which he was writing, he is reasonably frank. But there is not a trace in him of the feeling that one finds in *Manon Lescaut*, *Salammbô*, *Carmen*, *Wuthering Heights*. According to Aldous Huxley, D. H. Lawrence once said that Balzac was 'a gigantic dwarf', and in a sense the same is true of Dickens. There are whole worlds which he either knows nothing about or does not wish to mention. Except in a rather roundabout way, one cannot *learn* very much from Dickens. And to say this is to think almost immediately of the great Russian novelists of the nineteenth century. Why is it that Tolstoy's grasp seems to be so much larger than Dickens's – why is it that he seems able to tell you so much more *about yourself*? It is not that he is more gifted, or even, in the last analysis, more intelligent. It is because he is writing about people who are growing. His characters are struggling to make their souls, whereas Dickens's are already finished and perfect. In my own mind Dickens's people are present far more often and far more vividly than Tolstoy's, but always in a single unchangeable attitude, like pictures or pieces of furniture. You cannot hold an imaginary conversation with a Dickens character as you can with, say, Peter Bezoukhov. And this is not merely because of Tolstoy's greater seriousness, for there are also comic characters that you can imagine yourself talking to – Bloom, for instance, or Pécuchet, or even Wells's Mr Polly. It is because Dickens's characters have no mental life. They say perfectly the thing that they have to say, but they cannot be conceived as talking about anything else. They never learn, never speculate. Perhaps the most meditative of his characters is Paul Dombey, and his thoughts are mush. Does this mean that Tolstoy's novels are 'better' than Dickens's? The truth is that it is absurd to make such comparisons in terms of 'better' and 'worse'. If I were forced to compare Tolstoy with Dickens, I should say that Tolstoy's appeal will probably be wider in the long run, because Dickens is scarcely intelligible outside the English-speaking culture; on the other hand, Dickens is able to reach simple people, which Tolstoy is not. Tolstoy's characters can cross a frontier, Dickens can be portrayed on a cigarette-card. But one is no more obliged to choose between them than between a sausage and a rose. Their purposes barely intersect.

VI

If Dickens had been *merely* a comic writer, the chances are that no one would now remember his name. Or at best a few of his books would survive in rather the same way as books like *Frank Fairleigh, Mr Verdant Green* and *Mrs Caudle's Curtain Lectures*, as a sort of hangover of the Victorian atmosphere, a pleasant little whiff of oysters and brown stout. Who has not felt sometimes that it was 'a pity' that Dickens ever deserted the vein of *Pickwick* for things like *Little Dorrit* and *Hard Times*? What people always demand of a popular novelist is that he shall write the same book over and over again, forgetting that a man who would write the same book twice could not even write it once. Any writer who is not utterly lifeless moves upon a kind of parabola, and the downward curve is implied in the upper one. Joyce has to start with the frigid competence of *Dubliners* and end with the dream-language of *Finnegan's Wake*, but *Ulysses* and *Portrait of the Artist* are part of the trajectory. The thing that drove Dickens forward into a form of art for which he was not really suited, and at the same time caused us to remember him, was simply the fact that he was a moralist, the consciousness of 'having something to say'. He is always preaching a sermon, and that is the final secret of his inventiveness. For you can only create if you can *care*. Types like Squeers and Micawber could not have been produced by a hack writer looking for something to be funny about. A joke worth laughing at always has an idea behind it, and usually a subversive idea. Dickens is able to go on being funny because he is in revolt against authority, and authority is always there to be laughed at. There is always room for one more custard pie.

His radicalism is of the vaguest kind, and yet one always knows that it is there. That is the difference between being a moralist and a politician. He has no constructive suggestions, not even a clear grasp of the nature of the society he is attacking, only an emotional perception that something is wrong, all he can finally say is, 'Behave decently', which, as I suggested earlier, is not necessarily so shallow as it sounds. Most revolutionaries are potential Tories, because they imagine that everything can be put right by altering the *shape* of society; once that change is effected, as it sometimes is, they see no need for any other. Dickens has not this kind of mental coarseness. The vagueness of his discontent is the mark of its permanence. What he is out against is not this or that institution, but, as Chesterton put it, 'an expression on the human face'. Roughly speaking, his morality is the Christian morality, but in spite of his Anglican upbringing he was essentially a Bible-Christian, as he took care to make plain when writing his will. In any case he cannot properly be described as a religious man. He 'believed', undoubtedly, but religion in the devotional sense does not seem to have entered much into his thoughts.* Where he is Christian is in his quasi-instinctive siding with the oppressed against the oppressors. As a matter of course he is on the side of the underdog, always and everywhere. To carry this to its logical conclusion one has got to change sides when the underdog becomes an upperdog, and in fact Dickens does tend to do so. He loathes the Catholic Church, for instance, but as soon as the Catholics are persecuted (*Barnaby Rudge*) he is on their side. He loathes the aristocratic class even more, but as soon as they are really overthrown (the revolutionary chapters in *A Tale of Two Cities*) his sympathies swing round. Whenever he departs from this emotional attitude he goes astray. A well-known example is at the ending of *David Copperfield*, in which everyone who reads it feels that something has gone wrong. What is wrong is that the closing chapters are pervaded, faintly but not noticeably, by the cult of success. It is the gospel according to Smiles, instead of the gospel according to Dickens. The attractive, out-at-elbow characters are got rid of, Micawber makes a fortune, Heep gets into prison – both of these events are flagrantly impos-

* From a letter to his youngest son (in 1868): 'You will remember that you have never at home been harassed about religious observances, or mere formalities. I have always been anxious not to weary my children with such things, before they are old enough to form opinions respecting them. You will therefore understand the better that I now most solemnly impress upon you the truth and beauty of the Christian Religion, as it came from Christ Himself, and the impossibility of your going far wrong if you humbly but heartily respect it. . . . Never abandon the wholesome practice of saying your own private prayers, night and morning. I have never abandoned it myself, and I know the comfort of it.'

sible – and even Dora is killed off to make way for Agnes. If you like, you can read Dora as Dickens's wife and Agnes as his sister-in-law, but the essential point is that Dickens has 'turned respectable' and done violence to his own nature. Perhaps that is why Agnes is the most disagreeable of his heroines, the real legless angel of Victorian romance, almost as bad as Thackeray's Laura.

No grown-up person can read Dickens without feeling his limitations, and yet there does remain his native generosity of mind, which acts as a kind of anchor and nearly always keeps him where he belongs. It is probably the central secret of his popularity. A good-tempered antinomianism rather of Dickens's type is one of the marks of Western popular culture. One sees it in folk-stories and comic songs, in dream-figures like Mickey Mouse and Pop-eye the Sailor (both of them variants of Jack the Giant-killer), in the history of working-class Socialism, in the popular protests (always ineffective but not always a sham) against imperialism, in the impulse that makes a jury award excessive damages when a rich man's car runs over a poor man; it is the feeling that one is always on the wrong side of the underdog, on the side of the weak against the strong. In one sense it is a feeling that is fifty years out of date. The common man is still living in the mental world of Dickens, but nearly every modern intellectual has gone over to some or other form of totalitarianism. From the Marxist or Fascist point of view, nearly all that Dickens stands for can be written off as 'bourgeois morality'. But in moral outlook no one could be more 'bourgeois' than the English working classes. The ordinary people in the Western countries have never entered, mentally, into the world of 'realism' and power-politics. They may do so before long, in which case Dickens will be as out of date as the cab-horse. But in his own age and ours he has been popular chiefly because he was able to express in a comic, simplified and therefore memorable form the native decency of the common man. And it is important that from this point of view people of very different types can be described as 'common'. In a country like England, in spite of its class-structure, there does exist a certain cultural unity. All through the Christian ages, and especially since the French Revolution, the Western world has been haunted by the idea of freedom and equality; it is only an *idea*, but it has penetrated to all ranks of society. The most atrocious injustices, cruelties, lies, snobberies exist everywhere, but there are not many people who can regard these things with the same indifference as, say, a Roman slave-owner. Even the millionaire suffers from a vague sense of guilt, like a dog eating a stolen leg of mutton. Nearly everyone, whatever his actual conduct may be, responds emotionally to the idea of human brotherhood. Dickens voiced a code which was and on the whole still is believed in, even by people who violate it. It is difficult otherwise to explain why he could be both read by working people (a thing that has happened to no other novelist of his stature) and buried in Westminster Abbey.

When one reads any strongly individual piece of writing, one has the impression of seeing a face somewhere behind the page. It is not necessarily the actual face of the writer. I feel this very strongly with Swift, with Defoe, with Fielding, Stendhal, Thackeray, Flaubert, though in several cases I do not know what these people looked like and do not want to know. What one sees is the face that the writer *ought* to have. Well, in the case of Dickens I see a face that is not quite the face of Dickens's photographs, though it resembles it. It is the face of a man of about forty, with a small beard and a high colour. He is laughing, with a touch of anger in his laughter, but no triumph, no malignity. It is the face of a man who is always fighting against something, but who fights in the open and is not frightened, the face of a man who is *generously angry* – in other words, of a nineteenth-century liberal, a free intelligence, a type hated with equal hatred by all the smelly little orthodoxies which are now contending for our souls.

1939

The Art of Donald McGill

Who does not know the 'comics' of the cheap stationers' windows, the penny or twopenny coloured post cards with their endless succession of fat women in tight bathing-dresses and their crude drawing and unbearable colours, chiefly hedge-sparrow's-egg tint and Post Office red?

This question ought to be rhetorical, but it is curious fact that many people seem to be unaware of the existence of these things, or else to have a vague notion that they are something to be found only at the seaside, like nigger minstrels or peppermint rock. Actually they are on sale everywhere – they can be bought at nearly any Woolworth's, for example – and they are evidently produced in enormous numbers, new series constantly appearing. They are not to be confused with the various other types of comic illustrated post card, such as the sentimental ones dealing with puppies and kittens or the Wendyish, sub-pornographic ones which exploit the love affairs of children. They are a *genre* of their own, specializing in very 'low' humour, the mother-in-law, baby's-nappy, policemen's-boot type of joke, and distinguishable from all the other kinds by having no artistic pretensions. Some half-dozen publishing houses issue them, though the people who draw them seem not to be numerous at any one time.

I have associated them especially with the name of Donald McGill because he is not only the most prolific and by far the best of contemporary post card artists, but also the most representative, the most perfect in the tradition. Who Donald

McGill is, I do not know. He is apparently a trade name, for at least one series of post cards is issued simply as 'The Donald McGill Comics', but he is also unquestionable a real person with a style of drawing which is recognizable at a glance. Anyone who examines his post cards in bulk will notice that many of them are not despicable even as drawings, but it would be mere dilettantism to pretend that they have any direct aesthetic value. A comic post card is simply an illustration to a joke, invariably a 'low' joke, and it stands or falls by its ability to raise a laugh. Beyond that it has only 'ideological' interest. McGill is a clever draughtsman with a real caricaturist's touch in the drawing of faces, but the special value of his post cards is that they are so completely typical. They represent, as it were, the norm of the comic post card. Without being in the least imitative, they are exactly what comic post cards have been any time these last forty years, and from them the meaning and purpose of the whole *genre* can be inferred.

Get hold of a dozen of these things, preferably McGill's – if you pick out from a pile the ones that seem to you funniest, you will probably find that most of them are McGill's – and spread them out on a table. What do you see?

Your first impression is of overpowering vulgarity. This is quite apart from the ever-present obscenity, and apart also from the hideousness of the colours. They have an utter lowness of mental atmosphere which comes out not only in the nature of the jokes but, even more, in the grotesque, staring, blatant quality of the drawings. The designs, like those of a child, are full of heavy lines and empty spaces, and all the figures in them, every gesture and attitude, are deliberately ugly, the faces grinning and vacuous, the women monstrously paradied, with bottoms like Hottentots. Your second impression, however, is of indefinable familiarity. What do these things remind you of? What are they so like? In the first place, of course, they remind you of the barely different post cards which you probably gazed at in your childhood. But more than this, what you are really looking at is something as traditional as Greek tragedy, a sort of sub-world of smacked bottoms and scrawny mothers-in-law which is a part of Western European consciousness. Not that the jokes, taken one by one, are necessarily stale. Not being debarred from smuttiness, comic post cards repeat themselves less often than the joke columns in reputable magazines, but their basic subject-matter, the *kind* of joke they are aiming at, never varies. A few are genuinely witty, in a Max Millerish style. Examples:

'I like seeing experienced girls home.'
'But I'm not experienced!'
'You're not home yet!'

'I've been struggling for years to get a fur coat. How did you get yours?'
'I left off struggling.'

JUDGE: 'You are prevaricating, sir. Did you or did you not sleep with this woman?'
CO-RESPONDENT: 'Not a wink, my lord!'

In general, however, they are not witty, but humorous, and it must be said for McGill's post cards, in particular, that the drawing is often a good deal funnier than the joke beneath it. Obviously the outstanding characteristic of comic cards is their obscenity, and I must discuss that more fully later. But I give here a rough analysis of their habitual subject-matter, with such explanatory remarks as seem to be needed:

Sex. – More than half, perhaps three-quarters, of the jokes are sex jokes, ranging from the harmless to the all but unprintable. First favourite is probably the illegitimate baby. Typical captions : 'Could you exchange this lucky charm for a baby's feeding-bottle ?' 'She didn't ask me to the christening, so I'm not going to the wedding.' Also newlyweds, old maids, nude statues and women in bathing-dresses. All of these are *ipso facto* funny, mere mention of them being enough to raise a laugh. The cuckoldry joke is seldom exploited, and there are no references to homosexuality.

Conventions of the sex joke :

(i) Marriage only benefits women. Every man is plotting seduction and every woman is plotting marriage. No woman ever remained unmarried voluntarily.

(ii) Sex-appeal vanishes at about the age of twenty-five. Well-preserved and good-looking people beyond their first youth are never represented. The amorous honeymooning couple reappear as the grim-visaged wife and shapeless, moustachioed, red-nosed husband, no intermediate stage being allowed for.

Home life – Next to sex, the henpecked husband is the favourite joke. Typical caption : 'Did they get an X-ray of your wife's jaw at the hospital ?' – 'No, they got a moving picture instead.'

Conventions :

(i) There is no such thing as a happy marriage.

(ii) No man ever gets the better of a woman in argument.

Drunkenness – Both drunkenness and teetotalism are *ipso facto* funny.

Conventions :

(i) All drunken men have optical illusions.

(ii) Drunkenness is something peculiar to middle-aged men. Drunken youths or women are never represented.

W.C. jokes – There is not a large number of these. Chamber pots are *ipso facto* funny, and so are public lavatories. A typical post card captioned 'A Friend in Need', shows a man's hat blown off his head and disappearing down the steps of a ladies' lavatory.

Inter-working-class snobbery – Much in these post cards suggests that they are aimed at the better-off working class and poorer middle class. There are many jokes turning on malapropisms, illiteracy, dropped aitches and the rough manners of slum dwellers. Countless post cards show draggled hags of the stage-charwoman type exchanging 'unladylike' abuse. Typical repartee: 'I wish you were a statue and I was a pigeon!' A certain number produced since the war treat evacuation from the anti-evacuee angle. There are the usual jokes about tramps, beggars and criminals, and the comic maidservant appears fairly frequently. Also the comic navvy, bargee, etc.; but there are no anti-Trade-Union jokes. Broadly speaking, everyone with much over or much under £5 a week is regarded as laughable. The 'swell' is almost as automatically a figure of fun as the slum-dweller.

Stock figures – Foreigners seldom or never appear. The chief locality joke is the Scotsman, who is almost inexhaustible. The lawyer is always a swindler, the clergyman always a nervous idiot who says the wrong thing. The 'knut' or 'masher' still appears, almost as in Edwardian days, in out-of-date looking evening-clothes and an opera hat, or even spats and a knobby cane. Another survival is the Suffragette, one of the big jokes of the pre-1914 period and too valuable to be relinquished. She has reappeared, unchanged in physical appearance, as the Feminist lecturer or Temperance fanatic. A feature of the last few years is the complete absence of anti-Jew post cards. The 'Jew joke', always somewhat more ill-natured than the 'Scotch joke', disappeared abruptly soon after the rise of Hitler.

Politics – Any contemporary event, cult or activity which has comic possibilities (for example, 'free love', feminism, A.R.P., nudism) rapidly finds its way into the picture post cards, but their general atmosphere is extremely old-fashioned. The implied political outlook is a Radicalism appropriate to about the year 1900. At normal times they are not only not patriotic, but go in for a mild guying of patriotism, with jokes about 'God save the King', the Union Jack, etc. The European situation only began to reflect itself in them at some time in 1939, and first did so through the comic aspects of A.R.P. Even at this date few post cards mention the war except in A.R.P. jokes (fat woman stuck in the mouth of Anderson shelter: wardens neglecting their duty while young woman undresses at window she has forgotten to black out, etc., etc.) A few express anti-Hitler sentiments of a not very vindictive kind. One, not McGill's, shows Hitler with the usual hypertrophied backside, bending down to pick a flower. Caption: 'What would *you* do, chums?' This is about as high a flight of patriotism as any post card is likely to attain. Unlike the twopenny weekly papers, comic post cards are not the product of any great monopoly company, and evidently they are not regarded as having any importance in forming public opinion. There is no sign in them of any attempt to induce an outlook acceptable to the ruling class.

Here one comes back to the outstanding, all-important feature of comic post cards – their obscenity. It is by this that everyone remembers them, and it is also central to their purpose, though not in a way that is immediately obvious.

A recurrent, almost dominant motif in comic post cards is the woman with the stuck-out behind. In perhaps half of them, or more than half, even when the point of the joke has nothing to do with sex, the same female figure appears, a plump 'voluptuous' figure with the dress clinging to it as tightly as another skin and with breasts or buttocks grossly over-emphasized according to which way it is turned. There can be no doubt that these pictures lift the lid off a very widespread repression, natural enough in a country whose women when young tend to be slim to the point of skimpiness. But at the same time the McGill post card – and this applies to all other post cards in this *genre* – is not intended as pornography but, a subtler thing, as a skit on pornography. The Hottentot figures of the women are caricatures of the Englishman's secret ideal, not portraits of it. When one examines McGill's post cards more closely, one notices that his brand of humour only has a meaning in relation to a fairly strict moral code. Whereas in papers like *Esquire*, for instance, or *La Vie Parisienne*, the imaginary background of the jokes is always promiscuity, the utter breakdown of all standards, the background of the McGill post card is marriage. The four leading jokes are nakedness, illegitimate babies, old maids and newly married couples, none of which would seem funny in a really dissolute or even 'sophisticated' society. The post cards dealing with honeymoon couples always have the enthusiastic indecency of those village weddings where it is still considered screamingly funny to sew bells to the bridal bed. In one, for example, a young bridegroom is shown getting out of bed the morning after his wedding night. 'The first morning in our own little home, darling!' he is saying; 'I'll go and get the milk and paper and bring you up a cup of tea.' Inset is a picture of the front doorstep; on it are four newspapers and four bottles of milk. This is obscene, if you like, but it is not immoral. Its implication – and this is just the implication the *Esquire* or the *New Yorker* would avoid at all costs – is that marriage is something profoundly exciting and important, the biggest event in the average human being's life.

So also with jokes about nagging wives and tyrannous mothers-in-law. They do at least imply a stable society in which marriage is indissoluble and family loyalty taken for granted. And bound up with this is something I noted earlier, the fact there are no pictures, or hardly any, of good-looking people beyond their first youth. There is the 'spooning' couple and the middle-aged, cat-and-dog couple, but nothing in between. The liaison, the illicit but more or less decorous love-affair which used to be the stock joke of French comic papers, is not a post card subject. And this reflects, on a comic level, the working-class outlook which takes it as a matter of course that youth and adventure – almost, indeed, individual life – end with marriage. One of the few authentic class-differences, as opposed to class-distinctions, still existing in England is that the working classes age very much earlier. They do not live less long, provided that they survive their childhood, nor do they lose their physical activity earlier, but they do lose very early their youthful appearance. This fact is observable everywhere, but can be most easily verified by watching one of the higher age groups registering for military service; the middle- and upper-class members look, on average, ten years younger than the others. It is usual to attribute this to the harder lives that the working classes have to live, but it is doubtful whether any such difference now exists as would account for it. More probably the truth is that the working classes reach middle age earlier because they accept it earlier. For to look young after, say, thirty is largely a matter of wanting to do so. This generalization is less true of the better-paid workers, especially those who live in council houses and labour-saving flats, but it is true enough even of them to point to a difference of outlook. And in this, as usual, they are more traditional, more in accord with the Christian past than the well-to-do women who try to stay young at forty by means of physical-jerks, cosmetics and avoidance of child-bearing. The impulse to cling to youth at all costs, to attempt to preserve your sexual attraction, to see even in middle age a future for yourself and not merely for your children, is a thing of recent growth and has only precariously established itself. It will probably disappear again when our standard of living drops and our birth-rate rises. 'Youth's a stuff will not endure' expresses the normal, traditional attitude. It is this ancient wisdom that McGill and his colleagues are reflecting, no doubt unconsciously, when they allow for no transition stage between the honeymoon couple and those glamourless figures, Mum and Dad.

I have said that at least half of McGill's post cards are sex jokes, and a proportion, perhaps ten per cent, are far more obscene than anything else that is now printed in England. Newsagents are occasionally prosecuted for selling them, and there would be many more prosecutions if the broadest jokes were not invariably protected by double meanings. A single example will be enough to show how this is done. In one post card, captioned 'They didn't believe her', a young woman is demonstrating, with her hands held apart, something about two feet long to a couple of open-mouthed acquaintances. Behind her on the wall is a stuffed fish in a glass case, and beside that is a photograph of a nearly naked athlete. Obviously it is not the fish that she is referring to, but this could never be proved. Now, it is doubtful whether there is any paper in England that would print a joke of this kind, and certainly there is no paper that does so habitually. There is an immense amount of pornography of a mild sort, countless illustrated papers cashing in on women's legs, but there is no popular literature specializing in the 'vulgar', farcical aspect of sex. On the other hand, jokes exactly like McGill's are the ordinary small change of the revue and music-hall stage, and are also to be heard on the radio, at moments when the censor happens to be nodding. In England the gap between what can be said and what can be printed is rather exceptionally wide. Remarks and gestures which hardly anyone objects to on the stage would raise a public outcry if any attempt were made to reproduce them on paper. (Compare Max Miller's stage patter with his weekly column in the *Sunday Dispatch*.) The comic post cards are the only existing exception to this rule, the only medium in which really 'low' humour is considered to be printable. Only in post cards and on the variety stage can the stuck-out behind, dog and lamp-post, baby's nappy type of joke be freely exploited. Remembering that, one sees what function these post cards, in their humble way, are performing.

What they are doing is to give expression to the Sancho Panza view of life, the attitude to life that Miss Rebecca West once summed up as 'extracting as much fun as possible from smacking behinds in basement kitchens'. The Don Quixote-Sancho Panza combination, which of course is simply the ancient dualism of body and soul in fiction form, recurs more frequently in the literature of the last four hundred years than can be explained by mere imitation. It comes up again and again, in endless variations, Bouvard and Pécuchet, Jeeves and Wooster, Bloom and Dedalus, Holmes and Watson (the Holmes-Watson variant is an exceptionally subtle one, because the usual physical characteristics of two partners have been transposed). Evidently it corresponds to something enduring in our civilization, not in the sense that either character is to be found in a 'pure' state in real life, but in the sense that the two principles, noble folly and base wisdom, exist side by side in nearly every human being. If you look into your own mind, which are you, Don Quixote or Sancho Panza? Almost certainly you are both. There is one part of you that wishes to be a hero or a saint, but another part of you is a little fat man who sees very clearly the advantages of staying alive with a whole skin. He is your unofficial self, the voice of the belly protesting against the soul. His tastes lie towards safety, soft beds, no work, pots of beer and women with 'voluptuous' figures. He it is who punctures your fine attitudes and urges you to look after Number One, to be unfaithful to your wife, to bilk your debts, and so on and so forth. Whether you allow yourself to be influenced by him is a different question. But it is simply a lie to say that he is not part of you, just as it is a lie to say that Don Quixote is not part of you either, though most of what is said and written consists of one lie or the other, usually the first.

But though in varying forms he is one of the stock figures of literature, in real life, especially in the way society is ordered, his point of view never gets a fair hearing. There is a constant world-wide conspiracy to pretend that he is not there, or at least that he doesn't matter. Codes of law and morals, or religious systems, never have much room in them for a humorous view of life. Whatever is funny is subversive, every joke is ultimately a custard pie, and the reason why so large a proportion of jokes centre round obscenity is simply that all societies, as the price of survival, have to insist on a fairly high standard of sexual morality. A dirty joke is not, of course, a serious attack upon morality, but it is a sort of mental rebellion, a momentary wish that things were otherwise. So also with all other jokes, which always centre round cowardice, laziness, dishonesty or some other quality which society cannot afford to encourage. Society has always to demand a little more from human beings than it will get in practice. It has to demand faultless discipline and self-sacrifice, it must expect its subjects to work hard, pay their taxes, and be faithful to their wives, it must assume that men think it glorious to die on the battlefield and women want to wear themselves out with child-bearing. The whole of what one may call official literature is founded on such assumptions. I never read the proclamations of generals before battle, the speeches of führers and prime ministers, the solidarity songs of public schools and left-wing political parties, national anthems, Temperance tracts, papal encyclicals and sermons against gambling and contraception, without seeming to hear in the background a chorus of raspberries from all the millions of common men to whom these high sentiments make no appeal. Nevertheless the high sentiments always win in the end, leaders who offer blood, toil, tears and sweat always get more out of their followers than those who offer safety and a good time. When it comes to the pinch, human beings are heroic. Women face childbed and the scrubbing brush, revolutionaries keep their mouths shut in the torture chamber, battleships go down with their guns still firing when their decks are awash. It is only that the other element in man, the lazy, cowardly, debt-bilking adulterer who is inside all of us, can never be suppressed altogether and needs a hearing occasionally.

The comic post cards are one expression of his point of view, a humble one, less important than the music halls, but still worthy of attention. In a society which is still basically Christian they naturally concentrate on sex jokes; in a totalitarian society, if they had any freedom of expression at all, they would probably concentrate on laziness or cowardice, but at any rate on the unheroic in one form or another. It will not do to condemn them on the ground that they are vulgar and ugly. That is exactly what they are meant to be. Their whole meaning and virtue is in their unredeemed lowness, not only in the sense of obscenity, but lowness of outlook in every direction whatever. The slightest hint of 'higher' influences would ruin them utterly. They stand for the worm's-eye view of life, for the music-hall world where marriage is a dirty joke or a comic disaster, where the rent is always behind and the clothes are always up the spout, where the lawyer is always a crook and the Scotsman always a miser, where the newly-weds make fools of themselves on the hideous beds of seaside lodging-houses and the drunken, red-nosed husbands roll home at four in the morning to meet the linen-nightgowned wives who wait for them behind the front door, poker in hand. Their existence, the fact that people want them, is symptomatically important. Like the music halls, they are a sort of saturnalia, a harmless rebellion against virtue. They express only one tendency in the human mind, but a tendency which is always there and will find its own outlet, like water. On the whole, human beings want to be good, but not too good, and not quite all the time. For:

There is a just man that perished in his righteousness, and there is a wicked man that prolongeth his life in his wickedness. Be not righteous overmuch; neither make thyself over wise; why shouldst thou destroy thyself? Be not overmuch wicked, neither be thou foolish: why shouldst thou die before thy time?

In the past the mood of the comic post card could enter into the central stream of literature, and jokes barely different from McGill's could casually be uttered between the murders in Shakespeare's tragedies. That is no longer possible, and a whole category of humour, integral to our literature till 1800 or thereabouts, has dwindled down to these ill-drawn post cards, leading a barely legal existence in cheap stationers' windows. The corner of the human heart that they speak for might easily manifest itself in worse forms, and I for one should be sorry to see them vanish.

1941

Notes on Nationalism

Somewhere or other Byron makes use of the French word *longueur*, and remarks in passing that though in England we happen not to have the *word*, we have the *thing* in considerable profusion. In the same way, there is a habit of mind which is now so widespread that it affects our thinking on nearly every subject, but which has not yet been given a name. As the nearest existing equivalent I have chosen the word 'nationalism', but it will be seen in a moment that I am not using it in quite the ordinary sense, if only because the emotion I am speaking about does not always attach itself to what is called a nation – that is, a single race or a geographical area. It can attach itself to a church or class, or it may work in a merely negative sense, *against* something or other and without the need for any positive object of loyalty.

By 'nationalism' I mean first of all the habit of assuming that human beings can be classified like insects and that whole blocks of millions or tens of millions of people can be confidently labelled 'good' or 'bad'.* But secondly – and

---

* Nations, and even vaguer entities such as the Catholic Church or the proletariat, are commonly thought of as individuals and often referred to as 'she'. Patently absurd remarks such as 'Germany is naturally treacherous' are to be found in any newspaper one opens, and reckless generalizations about national character ('The Spaniard is a natural aristocrat' or 'Every Englishman is a hypocrite') are uttered by almost everyone. Intermittently these generalizations are seen to be unfounded, but the habit of making them persists, and people of professedly international outlook, e.g., Tolstoy or Bernard Shaw, are often guilty of them.

this is much more important – I mean the habit of identifying oneself with a single nation or other unit, placing it beyond good and evil and recognizing no other duty than that of advancing its interests. Nationalism is not be confused with patriotism. Both words are normally used in so vague a way that any definition is liable to be challenged, but one must draw a distinction between them, since two different and even opposing ideas are involved. By 'patriotism' I mean devotion to a particular place and a particular way of life, which one believes to be the best in the world but has no wish to force upon other people. Patriotism is of its nature defensive, both militarily and culturally. Nationalism, on the other hand, is inseparable from the desire for power. The abiding purpose of every nationalist is to secure more power and more prestige, *not* for himself but for the nation or other unit in which he has chosen to sink his own individuality.

So long as it is applied merely to the more notorious and identifiable nationalist movements in Germany, Japan, and other countries, all this is obvious enough. Confronted with a phenomenon like Nazism, which we can observe from the outside, nearly all of us would say much the same things about it. But here I must repeat what I said above, that I am only using the word 'nationalism' for lack of a better. Nationalism, in the extended sense in which I am using the word, includes such movements and tendencies as Communism, political Catholicism, Zionism, anti-Semitism, Trotskyism, and Pacifism. It does not necessarily mean loyalty to a government or a country, still less to *one's own* country, and it is not even strictly necessary that the units in which it deals should actually exist. To name a few obvious examples, Jewry, Islam, Christendom, the Proletariat, and the White Race are all of them the objects of passionate nationalistic feeling: but their existence can be seriously questioned, and there is no definition of any one of them that would be universally accepted.

It is also worth emphasizing once again that nationalist feeling can be purely negative. There are, for example, Trotskyists who have become simply the enemies of the U.S.S.R. without developing a corresponding loyalty to any other unit. When one grasps the implications of this, the nature of what I mean by nationalism becomes a good deal clearer. A nationalist is one who thinks solely, or mainly, in terms of competitive prestige. He may be a positive or a negative nationalist – that is, he may use his mental energy either in boosting or in denigrating – but at any rate his thoughts always turn on victories, defeats, triumphs, and humiliations. He sees history, especially contemporary history, as the endless rise and decline of great power units, and every event that happens seems to him a demonstration that his own side is on the up grade and some hated rival on the down grade. But finally, it is important not to confuse nationalism with mere worship of success. The nationalist does not go on the principle of simply ganging up with the strongest side. On the contrary, having picked his side, he persuades himself that it *is* the strongest, and is able to stick to his belief even when the facts are overwhelmingly against him. Nationalism is power-hunger tempered by self-deception. Every nationalist is capable of the most flagrant dishonesty, but he is also – since he is conscious of serving something bigger than himself – unshakably certain of being in the right.

Now that I have given this lengthy definition, I think it will be admitted that the habit of mind I am talking about is widespread among the English intelligentsia, and more widespread there than among the mass of the people. For those who feel deeply about contemporary politics, certain topics have become so infected by considerations of prestige that a genuinely rational approach to them is almost impossible. Out of the hundreds of examples that one might choose, take this question : Which of the three great allies, the U.S.S.R., Britain, and the U.S.A., has contributed most to the defeat of Germany ? In theory it should be possible to give a reasoned and perhaps even a conclusive answer to this question. In practice, however, the necessary calculations cannot be made, because anyone likely to bother his head about such a question would inevitably see it in terms of competitive prestige. He would therefore *start* by deciding in favour of Russia, Britain, or America as the case might be, and only *after* this would begin searching for arguments that seemed to support his case. And there are whole strings of kindred questions to which you can only get an honest answer from someone who is indifferent to the whole subject involved, and whose opinion on it is probably worthless in any case. Hence, partly, the remarkable failure in our time of political and military prediction. It is curious to reflect that out of all the 'experts' of all the schools, there was not a single one who was able to foresee so likely an event as the Russo-German pact of 1939.* And when the news of the Pact broke, the most wildly divergent explanations of it were given, and predictions were made which were falsified almost immediately, being based in nearly every case not on a study of probabilities but on a desire to make the U.S.S.R. seem good or bad, strong or weak. Political or military commentators, like astrologers, can survive almost any mistake, because their more devoted followers do not look to them for an appraisal of the facts but for the

---

* A few writers of conservative tendency, such as Peter Drucker, foretold an agreement between Germany and Russia, but they expected an actual alliance or amalgamation which would be permanent. No Marxist or other left-wing writer, of whatever colour, came anywhere near foretelling the Pact.

stimulation of nationalistic loyalties.* And aesthetic judgements, especially literary judgements, are often corrupted in the same way as political ones. It would be difficult for an Indian Nationalist to enjoy reading Kipling or for a Conservative to see merit in Mayakovsky, and there is always a temptation to claim that any book whose tendency one disagrees with must be a bad book from a *literary* point of view. People of strongly nationalist outlook often perform this sleight of hand without being conscious of dishonesty.

In England, if one simply considers the number of people involved, it is probable that the dominant form of nationalism is old-fashioned British jingoism. It is certain that this is still widespread, and much more so than most observers would have believed a dozen years ago. However, in this essay I am concerned chiefly with the reactions of the intelligentsia, among whom jingoism and even patriotism of the old kind are almost dead, though they now seem to be reviving among a minority. Among the intelligentsia, it hardly needs saying that the dominant form of nationalism is Communism – using this word in a very loose sense, to include not merely Communist Party members but 'fellow travellers' and Russophiles generally. A Communist, for my purpose

*The military commentators of the popular press can mostly be classified as pro-Russian or anti-Russian, pro-blimp or anti-blimp. Such errors as believing the Maginot Line impregnable, or predicting that Russia would conquer Germany in three months, have failed to shake their reputation, because they were always saying what their own particular audience wanted to hear. The two military critics most favoured by the intelligentsia are Captain Liddell Hart and Major-General Fuller, the first of whom teaches that the defence is stronger than the attack, and the second that the attack is stronger than the defence. This contradiction has not prevented both of them from being accepted as authorities by the same public. The secret reason for their vogue in left-wing circles is that both of them are at odds with the War Office.

here, is one who looks upon the U.S.S.R. as his Fatherland and feels it his duty to justify Russian policy and advance Russian interests at all costs. Obviously such people abound in England today, and their direct and indirect influence is very great. But many other forms of nationalism also flourish, and it is by noticing the points of resemblance between different and even seemingly opposed currents of thought that one can best get the matter into perspective.

Ten or twenty years ago, the form of nationalism most closely corresponding to Communism today was political Catholicism. Its most outstanding exponent – though he was perhaps an extreme case rather than a typical one – G. K. Chesterton. Chesterton was a writer of considerable talent who chose to suppress both his sensibilities and his intellectual honesty in the cause of Roman Catholic propaganda. During the last twenty years or so of his life, his entire output was in reality an endless repetition of the same thing, under its laboured cleverness as simple and boring as 'Great is Diana of the Ephesians'. Every book that he wrote, every paragraph, every sentence, every incident in every story, every scrap of dialogue, had to demonstrate beyond possibility of mistake the superiority of the Catholic over the Protestant or the pagan. But Chesterton was not content to think of this superiority as merely intellectual or spiritual : it had to be translated into terms of national prestige and military power, which entailed an ignorant idealization of the Latin countries, especially France. Chesterton had not lived long in France, and his picture of it – as a land of Catholic peasants incessantly singing the *Marseillaise* over glasses of red wine – had about as much relation to reality as *Chu Chin Chow* has to everyday life in Baghdad. And with this went not only an enormous overestimation of French military power (both before and after 1914–18 he maintained that France, by itself, was stronger than Germany), but a silly and vulgar glorification of the actual process of war. Chesterton's battle poems, such as *Lepanto* or *The Ballad of Saint Barbara*, make *The Charge of the Light Brigade* read like a pacifist tract: they are perhaps the most tawdry bits of bombast to be found in our language. The interesting thing is that had the romantic rubbish which he habitually wrote about France and the French army been written by somebody else about Britain and the British army, he would have been the first to jeer. In home politics he was a Little Englander, a true hater of jingoism and imperialism, and according to his lights a true friend of democracy. Yet when he looked outwards into the international field, he could forsake his principles without even noticing that he was doing so. Thus, his almost mystical belief in the virtues of democracy did not prevent him from admiring Mussolini. Mussolini had destroyed the representative government and the freedom of the Press for which Chesterton had struggled so hard at home, but Mussolini was an Italian and had made Italy strong, and that settled the matter. Nor did Chesteron ever find a word to say against imperialism and the conquest of coloured races when they were practised by Italians or Frenchmen. His hold on reality, his literary taste, and even to some extent his moral sense, were dislocated as soon as his nationalistic loyalties were involved.

Obviously there are considerable resemblances between political Catholicism as exemplified by Chesterton, and Communism. So there are between either of these and, for instance, Scottish Nationalism, Zionism, anti-Semitism or Trotskyism. It would be an over-simplification to say that all forms of nationalism are the same, even in their mental atmosphere, but there are certain rules that hold good in all cases. The following are the principal characteristics of nationalist thought:

Obsession. As nearly as possible, no nationalist ever thinks, talks, or writes about anything except the superiority of his own power unit. It is difficult if not impossible for any nationalist to conceal his allegiance. The smallest slur upon his own unit, or any implied praise of a rival organization, fills him with uneasiness which he can only relieve by making some sharp retort. If the chosen unit is an actual country, such as Ireland or India, he will generally claim superiority for it not only in military power and political virtue, but in art, literature, sport, the structure of the language, the physical beauty of the inhabitants, and perhaps even in climate, scenery and cooking. He will show great sensitiveness about such things as the correct display of flags, relative size of headlines and the order in which different countries are named.* Nomenclature plays a very important part in nationalist thought. Countries which have won their independence or gone through a nationalist revolution usually change their names, and any country or other unit round which strong feelings revolve is likely to have several names, each of them carrying a different implication. The two sides in the Spanish Civil War had between them nine or ten names expressing different degrees of love and hatred. Some of these names (e.g. 'Patriots' for Franco-supporters, or 'Loyalists' for Government-supporters) were frankly question-begging, and there was no single one of them which the two rival factions could have agreed to use. All nationalists consider it a duty to spread their own language to the detriment of rival languages, and among English-speakers this struggle reappears in subtler forms as a struggle between dialects. Anglophobe Americans will refuse to use a slang phrase if they know it to be of British origin, and the conflict between Latinizers and Germanizers often has nationalist motives behind it.

* Certain Americans have expressed dissatisfaction because 'Anglo-American' is the form of combination for these two words. It has been proposed to substitute 'Americo-British'.

Scottish nationalists insist on the superiority of Lowland Scots, and socialists whose nationalism takes the form of class hatred tirade against the B.B.C. accent and even the broad A. One could multiply instances. Nationalist thought often gives the impression of being tinged by belief in sympathetic magic – a belief which probably comes out in the widespread custom of burning political enemies in effigy, or using pictures of them as targets in shooting galleries.

Instability. The intensity with which they are held does not prevent nationalist loyalties from being transferable. To begin with, as I have pointed out already, they can be and often are fastened upon some foreign country. One quite commonly finds that great national leaders, or the founders of nationalist movements, do not even belong to the country they have glorified. Sometimes they are outright foreigners, or more often they come from peripheral areas where nationality is doubtful. Examples are Stalin, Hitler, Napoleon, de Valera, Disraeli, Poincaré, Beaverbrook. The Pan-German movement was in part the creation of an Englishman, Houston Chamberlain. For the past fifty or a hundred years, transferred nationalism has been a common phenomenon among literary intellectuals. With Lafcadio Hearne the transference was to Japan, with Carlyle and many others of his time to Germany, and in our own age it is usually Russia. But the peculiarly interesting fact is that *re*-transference is also possible. A country or other unit which has been worshipped for years may suddenly become detestable, and some other object of affection may take its place with almost no interval. In the first version of H. G. Wells's *Outline of History*, and others of his writings about that time, one finds the United States praised almost as extravagantly as Russia is praised by Communists today : yet within a few years this uncritical admiration had turned into hostility. The bigoted Communist who changes in a space of weeks, or even of days into an equally bigoted Trotskyist is a common spectacle. In continental Europe Fascist movements were largely recruited from among Communists, and the opposite process may well happen within the next few years. What remains constant in the nationalist is his own state of mind: the object of his feelings is changeable, and may be imaginary.

But for an intellectual, transference has an important function which I have already mentioned shortly in connexion with Chesterton. It makes it possible for him to be much *more* nationalistic – more vulgar, more silly, more malignant, more dishonest – than he could ever be on behalf of his native country, or any unit of which he had real knowledge. When one sees the slavish or boastful rubbish that is written about Stalin, the Red Army, etc., by fairly intelligent and sensitive people, one realizes that this is only possible because some kind of dislocation has taken place. In societies such as ours, it is unusual for anyone describable as an intellectual to feel a very deep attachment to his own country. Public opinion – that is, the section of public opinion of which he as an intellectual is aware – will not allow him to do so. Most of the people surrounding him are sceptical and disaffected, and he may adopt the same attitude from imitativeness or sheer cowardice: in that case he will have abandoned the form of nationalism that lies nearest to hand without getting any closer to a genuinely internationalist outlook. He still feels the need for a Fatherland, and it is natural to look for one somewhere abroad. Having found it, he can wallow unrestrainedly in exactly those emotions from which he believes that he has emancipated himself. God, the King, the Empire, the Union Jack – all the overthrown idols can reappear under different names, and because they are not recognised for what they are they can be worshipped with a good conscience. Transferred nationalism, like the use of scapegoats, is a way of attaining salvation without altering one's conduct.

Indifference to Reality. All nationalists have the power of not seeing resemblances between similar sets of facts. A British Tory will defend self-determination in Europe and oppose it in India with no feeling of inconsistency. Actions are held to be good or bad, not on their own merits but according to who does them, and there is almost no kind of outrage – torture, the use of hostages, forced labour, mass deportations, imprisonment without trial, forgery, assassination, the bombing of civilians – which does not change its moral colour when it is committed by 'our' side. The Liberal *News Chronicle* published, as an example of shocking barbarity, photographs of Russians hanged by the Germans, and then a year or two later published with warm approval almost exactly similar photographs of Germans hanged by the Russians.* It is the same with historical events. History is thought of largely in nationalist terms, and such things as the Inquisition, the tortures of the Star Chamber, the exploits of the English buccaneers (Sir Francis Drake, for instance, who was given to skinning Spanish prisoners alive), the Reign of Terror, the heroes of the Mutiny blowing hundreds of Indians from the guns, or Cromwell's soldiers slashing Irish women's faces with razors, become morally neutral or even meritorious when it is felt that they were done in 'the right' cause. If one looks back over the past quarter of a century, one finds that there was hardly a single year when atrocity stories were not being reported from some part of

* The *News Chronicle* advised its readers to visit the news film at which the entire execution could be witnessed, with close-ups. The *Star* published with seeming approval photographs of nearly naked female collaborationists being baited by the Paris mob. These photographs had a marked resemblance to the Nazi photographs of Jews being baited by the Berlin mob.

the world': and yet in not one single case were these atrocities – in Spain, Russia, China, Hungary, Mexico, Amritsar, Smyrna – believed in and disapproved of by the English intelligentsia as a whole. Whether such deeds were reprehensible, or even whether they happened, was always decided according to political predilection.

The nationalist not only does not disapprove of atrocities committed by his own side, but he has a remarkable capacity for not even hearing about them. For quite six years the English admirers of Hitler contrived not to learn of the existence of Dachau and Buchenwald. And those who were loudest in denouncing the German concentration camps were often quite unaware, or only very dimly aware, that there are also concentration camps in Russia. Huge events like the Ukraine famine of 1933, involving the deaths of millions of people, have actually escaped the attention of the majority of English Russophiles. Many English people heard almost nothing about the extermination of German and Polish Jews during the war. Their own anti-Semitism has caused this vast crime to bounce off their consciousness. In nationalist thought there are facts which are both true and untrue, known and unknown. A known fact may be so unbearable that it is habitually pushed aside and not allowed to enter into logical processes, or on the other hand it may enter into every calculation and yet never be admitted as a fact, even in one's own mind.

Every nationalist is haunted by the belief that the past can be altered. He spends part of his time in a fantasy world in which things happen as they should – in which, for example, the Spanish Armada was a success or the Russian Revolution was crushed in 1918 – and he will transfer fragments of this world to the history books whenever possible. Much of the propagandist writing of our time amounts to plain forgery. Material facts are suppressed, dates altered, quotations removed from their context and doctored so as to change their meaning. Events which, it is felt, ought not to have happened are left unmentioned and ultimately denied.* In 1927 Chiang Kai-shek boiled hundreds of Communists alive, and yet within ten years he had become one of the heroes of the Left. The realignment of world politics had brought him into the anti-Fascist camp, and so it was felt that the boiling of the Communists 'didn't count', or perhaps had not happened. The primary aim of propaganda is, of course, to influence contemporary opinion, but those who rewrite history do probably believe with part of their minds that they are actually thrusting facts into the past. When one considers the elaborate forgeries that have been committed in order to show that Trotsky did not play a valuable part in the Russian civil war, it is difficult to feel that the people responsible are merely lying. More probably they feel that their own version *was* what happened in the sight of God, and that one is justified in re-arranging the records accordingly.

Indifference to objective truth is encouraged by the sealing-off of one part of the world from another, which makes it harder and harder to discover what is actually happening. There can often be a genuine doubt about the most enormous events. For example, it is impossible to calculate within millions, perhaps even tens of millions, the number of deaths caused by the war. The calamities that were constantly being reported – battles, massacres, famines, revolutions – tended to inspire in the average person a feeling of unreality. One had no way of verifying the facts, one was not even fully certain that they had happened, and one was always presented with totally different interpretations from different

* An example is the Russo-German Pact, which is being effaced as quickly as possible from public memory. A Russian correspondent informs me that mention of the Pact is already being omitted from Russian year-books which table recent political events.

sources. What were the rights and wrongs of the Warsaw Rising of August 1944? Was it true about the German gas ovens in Poland? Who was really to blame for the Bengal famine? Probably the truth is discoverable, but the facts will be so dishonestly set forth in almost any newspaper that the ordinary reader can be forgiven either for swallowing lies or for failing to form an opinion. The general uncertainty as to what is really happening makes it easier to cling to lunatic beliefs. Since nothing is ever quite proved or disproved, the most unmistakable fact can be impudently denied. Moreover, although endlessly brooding on power, victory, defeat, revenge, the nationalist is often somewhat uninterested in what happens in the real world. What he wants is to *feel* that his own unit is getting the better of some other unit, and he can more easily do this by scoring off an adversary than by examining the facts to see whether they support him. All nationalist controversy is at the debating-society level. It is almost entirely inconclusive, since each contestant invariably believes himself to have won the victory. Some nationalists are not far from schizophrenia, living quite happily amid dreams of power and conquest which have no connexion with the physical world.

I have examined as best I can the mental habits which are common to all forms of nationalism. The next thing is to classify those forms, but obviously this cannot be done comprehensively. Nationalism is an enormous subject. The world is tormented by innumerable delusions and hatreds which cut across one another in an extremely complex way, and some of the most sinister of them have not yet even impinged on the European consciousness. In this essay I am concerned with nationalism as it occurs among the English intelligentsia. In them, much more often than in ordinary English people, it is unmixed with patriotism and can therefore be studied pure. Below are listed the varieties of nationalism now flourishing among English intellectuals, with such comments as seem to be needed. It is convenient to use three headings, Positive, Transferred, and Negative, though some varieties will fit into more than one category :

Positive Nationalism

(i) *Neo-Toryism*. Exemplified by such people as Lord Elton, A. P. Herbert, G. M. Young, Professor Pickthorne, by the literature of the Tory Reform Committee, and by such magazines as the *New English Review* and the *Nineteenth Century and After*. The real motive force of Neo-Toryism, giving it its nationalistic character and differentiating it from ordinary Conservatism, is the desire not to recognize that British power and influence have declined. Even those who are realistic enough to see that Britain's military position is not what it was, tend to claim that 'English ideas' (usually left undefined) must dominate the world. All Neo-Tories are anti-Russian, but sometimes the main emphasis is anti-American. The significant thing is that this school of thought seems to be gaining ground among youngish intellectuals, sometimes ex-Communists, who have passed through the usual process of disillusionment and become disillusioned with that. The Anglophobe who suddenly becomes violently pro-British is a fairly common figure. Writers who illustrate this tendency are F. A. Voigt, Malcolm Muggeridge, Evelyn Waugh, Hugh Kingsmill, and a psychologically similar development can be observed in T. S. Eliot, Wyndham Lewis, and various of their followers.

(ii) *Celtic Nationalism*. Welsh, Irish, and Scottish nationalism have points of difference but are alike in their anti-English orientation. Members of all three movements opposed the war while continuing to describe themselves as pro-Russian, and the lunatic fringe even contrived to be sim-ultaneously pro-Russian and pro-Nazi. But Celtic nationalism is not the same thing as Anglophobia. Its motive force is a belief in the past and future greatness of the Celtic peoples, and it has a strong tinge of racialism. The Celt is supposed to be spiritually superior to the Saxon – simpler, more creative, less vulgar, less snobbish, etc. – but the usual power-hunger is there under the surface. One symptom of it is the delusion that Eire, Scotland, or even Wales could preserve its independence unaided and owes nothing to British protection. Among writers, good examples of this school of thought are Hugh McDiarmid and Sean O'Casey. No modern Irish writer, even of the stature of Yeats or Joyce, is completely free from traces of nationalism.

(iii) *Zionism*. This has the usual characteristics of a nation-alist movement, but the American variant of it seems to be more violent and malignant than the British. I classify it under Direct and not Transferred nationalism because it flourishes almost exclusively among the Jews themselves. In England, for several rather incongruous reasons, the intelli-gentsia are mostly pro-Jew on the Palestine issue, but they do not feel strongly about it. All English people of good will are also pro-Jew in the sense of disapproving of Nazi perse-cution. But any actual nationalistic loyalty, or belief in the innate superiority of Jews, is hardly to be found among Gentiles.

Transferred Nationalism

(i) *Communism*.

(ii) *Political Catholicism*.

(iii) *Colour Feeling*. The old-style contemptuous attitude towards 'natives' has been much weakened in England, and various pseudo-scientific theories emphasizing the superiority of the white race have been abandoned.* Among the intelligentsia, colour feeling only occurs in the transposed form, that is, as a belief in the innate superiority of the coloured races. This is now increasingly common among English intellectuals, probably resulting more often from masochism and sexual frustration than from contact with the Oriental and Negro nationalist movements. Even among those who do not feel strongly on the colour question, snobbery and imitation have a powerful influence. Almost any English intellectual would be scandalized by the claim that the white races are superior to the coloured, whereas the opposite claim would seem to him unexceptionable even if he disagreed with it. Nationalistic attachment to the coloured races is usually mixed up with the belief that their sex lives are superior, and there is a large underground mythology about the sexual prowess of Negroes.

(iv) *Class Feeling.* Among upper-class and middle-class intellectuals, only in the transposed form – i.e. as a belief in the superiority of the proletariat. Here again, inside the intelligentsia, the pressure of public opinion is overwhelming. Nationalistic loyalty towards the proletariat, and most vicious theoretical hatred of the bourgeoisie, can and often do co-exist with ordinary snobbishness in everyday life.

(v) *Pacifism.* The majority of pacifists either belong to obscure religious sects or are simply humanitarians who

*A good example is the sunstroke superstition. Until recently it was believed that the white races were much more liable to sunstroke than the coloured, and that a white man could not safely walk about in tropical sunshine without a pith helmet. There was no evidence whatever for this theory, but it served the purpose of accentuating the difference between 'natives' and Europeans. During the war the theory was quietly dropped and whole armies manoeuvred in the tropics without pith helmets. So long as the sunstroke superstition survived, English doctors in India appear to have believed in it as firmly as laymen.

object to taking life and prefer not to follow their thoughts beyond that point. But there is a minority of intellectual pacifists whose real though unadmitted motive appears to be hatred of Western democracy and admiration for totalitarianism. Pacifist propaganda usually boils down to saying that one side is as bad as the other, but if one looks closely at the writings of the younger intellectual pacifists, one finds that they do not by any means express impartial disapproval but are directed almost entirely against Britain and the United States. Moreover they do not as a rule condemn violence as such, but only violence used in defence of the Western countries. The Russians, unlike the British, are not blamed for defending themselves by warlike means, and indeed all pacifist propaganda of this type avoids mention of Russia or China. It is not claimed, again, that the Indians should abjure violence in their struggle against the British. Pacifist literature abounds with equivocal remarks which, if they mean anything, appear to mean that statesmen of the type of Hitler are preferable to those of the type of Churchill, and that violence is perhaps excusable if it is violent enough. After the fall of France, the French pacifists, faced by a real choice which their English colleagues have not had to make, mostly went over to the Nazis, and in England there appears to have been some small overlap of membership between the Peace Pledge Union and the Blackshirts. Pacifist writers have written in praise of Carlyle, one of the intellectual fathers of Fascism. All in all it is difficult not to feel that pacifism, as it appears among a section of the intelligentsia, is secretly inspired by an admiration for power and successful cruelty. The mistake was made of pinning this emotion to Hitler, but it could easily be re-transferred.

(i) *Anglophobia*. Within the intelligentsia, a derisive and mildly hostile attitude towards Britain is more or less compulsory, but it is an unfaked emotion in many cases. During the war it was manifested in the defeatism of the intelligentsia, which persisted long after it had become clear that the Axis powers could not win. Many people were undisguisedly pleased when Singapore fell or when the British were driven out of Greece, and there was a remarkable unwillingness to believe in good news, e.g. El Alamein, or the number of German planes shot down in the Battle of Britain. English left-wing intellectuals did not, of course, actually want the Germans or Japanese to win the war, but many of them could not help getting a certain kick out of seeing their own country humiliated, and wanted to feel that the final victory would be due to Russia, or perhaps America, and not to Britain. In foreign politics many intellectuals follow the principle that any faction backed by Britain must be in the wrong. As a result, 'enlightened' opinion is quite largely a mirror-image of Conservative policy. Anglophobia is always liable to reversal, hence that fairly common spectacle, the pacifist of one war who is a bellicist in the next.

(ii) *Anti-Semitism*. There is little evidence about this at present, because the Nazi persecutions have made it necessary for any thinking person to side with the Jews against their oppressors. Anyone educated enough to have heard the word 'anti-Semitism' claims as a matter of course to be free of it, and anti-Jewish remarks are carefully eliminated from all classes of literature. Actually anti-Semitism appears to be widespread, even among intellectuals, and the general conspiracy of silence probably helps to exacerbate it. People of Left opinions are not immune to it, and their attitude is sometimes affected by the fact that Trotskyists and anarchists tend to be Jews. But anti-Semitism comes more naturally to people of Conservative tendency, who suspect the Jews of weakening national morale and diluting the national culture. Neo-Tories and political Catholics are always liable to succumb to anti-Semitism, at least intermittently.

(iii) *Trotskyism*. This word is used so loosely as to include anarchists, democratic Socialists and even Liberals. I use it here to mean a doctrinaire Marxist whose main motive is hostility to the Stalin régime. Trotskyism can be better studied in obscure pamphlets or in papers like the *Socialist Appeal* than in the works of Trotsky himself, who was by no means a man of one idea. Although in some places, for instance in the United States, Trotskyism is able to attract a fairly large number of adherents and develop into an organized movement with a petty führer of its own, its inspiration is essentially negative. The Trotskyist is *against* Stalin just as the Communist is *for* him, and, like the majority of Communists, he wants not so much to alter the external world as to feel that the battle for prestige is going in his own favour. In each case there is the same obsessive fixation on a single subject, the same inability to form a genuinely rational opinion based on probabilities. The fact that Trotskyists are everywhere a persecuted minority, and that the accusation usually made against them, i.e. of collaborating with the Fascists, is obviously false, creates an impression that Trotskyism is intellectually and morally superior to Communism; but it is doubtful whether there is much difference. The most typical Trotskyists, in any case, are ex-Communists, and no one arrives at Trotskyism except via one of the left-wing movements. No Communist, unless tethered to his party by years of habit, is secure against a sudden lapse into Trotskyism. The opposite process does not seem to happen equally often, though there is no clear reason why it should not.

In the classification I have attempted above, it will seem that I have often exaggerated, over-simplified, made unwarranted assumptions and left out of account the existence of ordinarily decent motives. This was inevitable, because in this essay I am trying to isolate and identify tendencies which exist in all our minds and pervert our thinking, without necessarily occurring in a pure state or operating continuously. It is important at this point to correct the over-simplified picture which I have been obliged to make. To begin with, one has no right to assume that *everyone*, or even every intellectual, is infected by nationalism. Secondly, nationalism can be intermittent and limited. An intelligent man may half-succumb to a belief which attracts him but which he knows to be absurd, and he may keep it out of his mind for long periods, only reverting to it in moments of anger or sentimentality, or when he is certain that no important issue is involved. Thirdly, a nationalistic creed may be adopted in good faith from non-nationalist motives. Fourthly, several kinds of nationalism, even kinds that cancel out, can co-exist in the same person.

All the way through I have said 'the nationalist does this' or 'the nationalist does that', using for purposes of illustration the extreme, barely sane type of nationalist who has no neutral areas in his mind and no interest in anything except the struggle for power. Actually such people are fairly common, but they are not worth powder and shot. In real life Lord Elton, D. N. Pritt, Lady Houston, Ezra Pound, Lord Vansittart, Father Coughlin and all the rest of their dreary tribe have to be fought against, but their intellectual deficiencies hardly need pointing out. Monomania is not interesting, and the fact that no nationalist of the more bigoted kind can write a book which still seems worth reading after a lapse of years has a certain deodorizing effect. But when one has admitted that nationalism has not triumphed everywhere, that there are still people whose judgements are not at the mercy of their desires, the fact does remain that the nationalistic habit of thought is widespread, so much so that various large and pressing problems – India, Poland, Palestine, the Spanish Civil War, the Moscow trials, the American Negroes, the Russo-German pact or what-have-you – cannot be, or at least never are, discussed upon a reasonable level. The Eltons and Pritts and Coughlins, each of them simply an enormous mouth bellowing the same lie over and over again, are obviously extreme cases, but we deceive ourselves if we do not realize that we can all resemble them in unguarded moments. Let a certain note be struck, let this or that corn be trodden on – and it may be a corn whose very existence has been unsuspected hitherto – and the most fairminded and sweet-tempered person may suddenly be transformed into a vicious partisan, anxious only to 'score' over his adversary and indifferent as to how many lies he tells or how many logical errors he commits in doing so. When Lloyd George, who was an opponent of the Boer War, announced in the House of Commons that the British communiqués, if one added them together, claimed the killing of more Boers than the whole Boer nation contained, it is recorded that Arthur Balfour rose to his feet and shouted 'Cad!' Very few people are proof against lapses of this type. The Negro snubbed by a white woman, the Englishman who hears England ignorantly criticized by an American, the Catholic apologist reminded of the Spanish Armada, will all react in much the same way. One prod to the nerve of nationalism, and the intellectual decencies can vanish, the past can be altered, and the plainest facts can be denied.

If one harbours anywhere in one's mind a nationalistic loyalty or hatred, certain facts, although in a sense known to be true, are inadmissible. Here are just a few examples. I list below five types of nationalist, and against each I append a fact which it is impossible for that type of nationalist to accept, even in his secret thoughts:

BRITISH TORY. Britain has come out of the war with reduced power and prestige.

COMMUNIST. If she had not been aided by Britain and America, Russia would have been defeated by Germany.

IRISH NATIONALIST. Eire can only remain independent because of British protection.

TROTSKYIST. The Stalin régime is accepted by the Russian masses.

PACIFIST. Those who 'abjure' violence can only do so because others are committing violence on their behalf.

All of these facts are grossly obvious if one's emotions do not happen to be involved: but to the kind of person named in each case they are also *intolerable*, and so they have to be denied, and false theories constructed upon their denial. I come back to the astonishing failure of military prediction in the war. It is, I think, true to say that the intelligentsia were more wrong about the progress of the war than the common people, and that they were precisely wrong because they were more swayed by partisan feelings. The average intellectual of the Left believed, for instance, that the war was lost in 1940, that the Germans were bound to overrun Egypt in 1942, that the Japanese would never be driven out of the lands they had conquered, and that the Anglo-American bombing offensive was making no impression on Germany. He could believe these things because his hatred of the British ruling class forbade him to admit that British plans could succeed. There is no limit to the follies that can be swallowed if one is under the influence of feelings of this kind. I have heard it confidently stated, for instance, that the American troops had been brought to Europe not to fight the Germans but to crush an English revolution. One has to belong to the intelligentsia to believe things like that: no ordinary man could be such a fool. When Hitler invaded Russia, the officials of the M.O.I. issued 'as background' a warning that Russia might be expected to collapse in six weeks. On the other hand the Communists regarded every phase of the war as a Russian victory, even when the Russians were driven back almost to the Caspian Sea and had lost several million prisoners. There is no need to multiply instances. The point is that as soon as fear, hatred, jealousy, and power-worship are involved, the sense of reality becomes unhinged. And, as I have pointed out already, the sense of right and wrong becomes unhinged also. There is no crime, absolutely none, that cannot be condoned when 'our' side commits it. Even if one does not deny that the crime has happened, even if one knows that it is exactly the same crime as one has condemned in some other case, even if one admits in an intellectual sense that it is unjustified – still one cannot *feel* that it is wrong. Loyalty is involved, and so pity ceases to function.

The reason for the rise and spread of nationalism is far too big a question to be raised here. It is enough to say that, in the forms in which it appears among English intellectuals, it is a distorted reflection of the frightful battles actually happening in the external world, and that its worst follies have been made possible by the breakdown of patriotism and religious belief. If one follows up this train of thought, one is in danger of being led into a species of Conservatism, or into political quietism. It can be plausibly argued, for instance – it is even probably true – that patriotism is an inoculation against nationalism, that monarchy is a guard against dictatorship, and that organized religion is a guard against superstition. Or again it can be argued that *no* unbiased outlook is possible, that *all* creeds and causes involve the same lies, follies, and barbarities; and this is often advanced as a reason for keeping out of politics altogether. I do not accept this argument, if only because in the modern world no one describable as an intellectual *can* keep out of politics in the sense of not caring about them. I think one must engage in politics – using the word in a wide sense – and that one must have preferences: that is, one must recognize that some causes are objectively better than others, even if they are advanced by equally bad means. As for the nationalistic loves and hatreds that I have spoken of, they are part of the make-up of most of us, whether we like it or not. Whether it is possible to get rid of them I do not know, but I do believe that it is possible to struggle against them, and that this is essentially a *moral* effort. It is a question first of all of discovering what one really is, what one's own feelings really are, and then of making allowance for the inevitable bias. If you hate and fear Russia, if you are jealous of the wealth and power of America, if you despise Jews, if you have a sentiment of inferiority towards the British ruling class, you cannot get rid of those feelings simply by taking thought. But you can at least recognize that you have them, and prevent them from contaminating your mental processes. The emotional urges which are inescapable, and are perhaps even necessary to political action, should be able to exist side by side with an acceptance of reality. But this, I repeat, needs a *moral* effort, and contemporary English literature, so far as it is alive at all to the major issues of our time, shows how few of us are prepared to make it.

1945

Why I Write

From a very early age, perhaps the age of five or six, I knew that when I grew up I should be a writer. Between the ages of about seventeen and twenty-four I tried to abandon this idea, but I did so with the consciousness that I was outraging my true nature and that sooner or later I should have to settle down and write books.

I was the middle child of three, but there was a gap of five years on either side, and I barely saw my father before I was eight. For this and other reasons I was somewhat lonely, and I soon developed disagreeable mannerisms which made me unpopular throughout my schooldays. I had the lonely child's habit of making up stories and holding conversations with imaginary persons, and I think from the very start my literary ambitions were mixed up with the feeling of being isolated and undervalued. I knew that I had a facility with words and a power of facing unpleasant facts, and I felt that this created a sort of private world in which I could get my own back for my failure in everyday life. Nevertheless the volume of serious – i.e. seriously intended – writing which I produced all through my childhood and boyhood would not amount to half a dozen pages. I wrote my first poem at the age of four or five, my mother taking it down to dictation. I cannot remember anything about it except that it was about a tiger and the tiger had 'chair-like teeth' – a good enough phrase, but I fancy the poem was a plagiarism of Blake's 'Tiger, Tiger'. At eleven when the war of 1914–18 broke out, I wrote a patriotic poem which was printed in the local newspaper, as was another, two years later, on the death of Kitchener. From time to time, when I was a bit older, I wrote bad and usually unfinished 'nature poems' in the Georgian style. I also, about twice, attempted a short story which was a ghastly failure. That was the total of the would-be serious work that I actually set down on paper during all those years.

However, throughout this time I did in a sense engage in literary activities. To begin with there was the made-to-order stuff which I produced quickly, easily and without much pleasure to myself. Apart from school work, I wrote *vers d'occasion*, semi-comic poems which I could turn out at what now seems to me astonishing speed – at fourteen I wrote a whole rhyming play, in imitation of Aristophanes, in about a week – and helped to edit school magazines, both printed and in manuscript. These magazines were the most pitiful burlesque stuff that you could imagine, and I took far less trouble with them than I now would with the cheapest journalism. But side by side with all this, for fifteen years or more, I was carrying out a literary exercise of a quite different kind: this was the making up of a continuous 'story' about myself, a sort of diary existing only in the mind. I believe this is a common habit of children and adolescents. As a very small child I used to imagine that I was, say, Robin Hood, and picture myself as the hero of thrilling adventures, but quite soon my 'story' ceased to be narcissistic in a crude way and became more and more a mere description of what I was doing and the things I saw. For minutes at a time this kind of thing would be running through my head: 'He pushed the door open and entered the room. A yellow beam of sunlight, filtering through the muslin curtains, slanted on to the table, where a matchbox, half open, lay beside the inkpot. With his right hand in his pocket he moved across to the window. Down in the street a tortoiseshell cat was chasing a dead leaf,' etc., etc. This habit continued till I was about twenty-five, right through my non-literary years. Although I had to search, and did search, for the right words, I seemed to be making this descriptive effort almost against my will, under a kind of compulsion from outside. The 'story' must, I suppose, have reflected the styles of the various writers I admired at different ages, but so far as I remember it always had the same meticulous descriptive quality.

When I was about sixteen I suddenly discovered the joy of mere words, i.e. the sounds and associations of words. The lines from *Paradise Lost* –

> So hee with difficulty and labour hard
> Moved on : with difficulty and labour hee,

which do not now seem to me so very wonderful, sent shivers down my backbone; and the spelling 'hee' for 'he' was an added pleasure. As for the need to describe things, I knew all about it already. So it is clear what kind of books I wanted to write, in so far as I could be said to want to write books at that time, I wanted to write enormous naturalistic novels with unhappy endings, full of detailed descriptions and arresting similes, and also full of purple passages in which words were used partly for the sake of their sound. And in fact my first completed novel, *Burmese Days*, which I wrote when I was thirty but projected much earlier, is rather that kind of book.

I give all this background information because I do not think one can assess a writer's motives without knowing something of his early development. His subject matter will be determined by the age he lives in – at least this is true in tumultuous, revolutionary ages like our own – but before he ever begins to write he will have acquired an emotional attitude from which he will never completely escape. It is his job, no doubt, to discipline his temperament and avoid getting stuck at some immature stage, or in some perverse mood : but if he escapes from his early influences altogether, he will have killed his impulse to write. Putting aside the need to earn a living, I think there are four great motives for writing, at any rate for writing prose. They exist in different degrees in every writer, and in any one writer the proportions will vary from time to time, according to the atmosphere in which he is living. They are :

(i) *Sheer egoism.* Desire to seem clever, to be talked about, to be remembered after death, to get your own back on grown-ups who snubbed you in childhood, etc., etc. It is humbug to pretend that this is not a motive, and a strong one. Writers share this characteristic with scientists, artists, politicians, lawyers, soldiers, successful business men – in short, with the whole top crust of humanity. The great mass of human beings are not acutely selfish. After the age of about thirty they abandon individual ambition – in many cases, indeed, they almost abandon the sense of being individuals at all – and live chiefly for others, or are simply smothered under drudgery. But there is also the minority of gifted, wilful people who are determined to live their own lives to the end, and writers belong in this class. Serious writers, I should say, are on the whole more vain and self-centred than journalists, though less interested in money.

(ii) *Aesthetic enthusiasm.* Perception of beauty in the external world, or, on the other hand, in words and their right arrangement. Pleasure in the impact of one sound on another, in the firmness of good prose or the rhythm of a good story. Desire to share an experience which one feels is valuable and ought not to be missed. The aesthetic motive is very feeble in a lot of writers, but even a pamphleteer or a writer of text-books will have pet words and phrases which appeal to him for non-utilitarian reasons; or he may feel strongly about typography, width of margins, etc. Above the level of a railway guide, no book is quite free from aesthetic considerations.

(iii) *Historical impulse*. Desire to see things as they are, to find out true facts and store them up for the use of posterity.

(iv) *Political purpose* – using the word 'political in the widest possible sense. Desire to push the world in a certain direction, to alter other people's idea of the kind of society that they should strive after. Once again, no book is genuinely free from political bias. The opinion that art should have nothing to do with politics is itself a political attitude.

It can be seen how these various impulses must war against one another, and how they must fluctuate from person to person and from time to time. By nature – taking your 'nature' to be the state you have attained when you are first adult – I am a person in whom the first three motives would outweigh the fourth. In a peaceful age I might have written ornate or merely descriptive books, and might have remained almost unaware of my political loyalties. As it is I have been forced into becoming a sort of pamphleteer. First I spent five years in an unsuitable profession (the Indian Imperial Police, in Burma), and then I underwent poverty and the sense of failure. This increased my natural hatred of authority and made me for the first time fully aware of the existence of the working classes, and the job in Burma had given me some understanding of the nature of imperialism : but these experiences were not enough to give me an accurate political orientation: Then came Hitler, the Spanish civil war, etc. By the end of 1935 I had still failed to reach a firm decision. I remember a little poem that I wrote at that date, expressing my dilemma :

> A happy vicar I might have been
> Two hundred years ago
> To preach upon eternal doom
> And watch my walnuts grow;

But born, alas, in an evil time,
I missed that pleasant haven,
For the hair has grown on my upper lip
And the clergy are all clean-shaven.

And later still the times were good,
We were so easy to please,
We rocked our troubled thoughts to sleep
On the bosoms of the trees.

All ignorant we dared to own
The joys we now dissemble;
The greenfinch on the apple bough
Could make my enemies tremble.

But girls' bellies and apricots,
Roach in a shaded stream,
Horses, ducks in flight at dawn,
All these are a dream.

It is forbidden to dream again;
We maim our joys or hide them;
Horses are made of chromium steel
And little fat men shall ride them.

I am the worm who never turned,
The eunuch without a harem;
Between the priest and the commissar
I walk like Eugene Aram;

And the commissar is telling my fortune
While the radio plays,
But the priest has promised an Austin Seven,
For Duggie always pays.

I dreamed I dwelt in marble halls,
And woke to find it true;
I wasn't born for an age like this;
Was Smith? Was Jones? Were you?

Why I Write

The Spanish war and other events in 1936–7 turned the scale and thereafter I knew where I stood. Every line of serious work that I have written since 1936 has been written, directly or indirectly, *against* totalitarianism and *for* democratic socialism, as I understand it. It seems to me nonsense, in a period like our own, to think that one can avoid writing of such subjects. Everyone writes of them in one guise or another. It is simply a question of which side one takes and what approach one follows. And the more one is conscious of one's political bias, the more chance one has of acting politically without sacrificing one's aesthetic and intellectual integrity.

What I have most wanted to do throughout the past ten years is to make political writing into an art. My starting point is always a feeling of partisanship, a sense of injustice. When I sit down to write a book, I do not say to myself, 'I am going to produce a work of art'. I write it because there is some lie that I want to expose, some fact to which I want to draw attention, and my initial concern is to get a hearing. But I could not do the work of writing a book, or even a long magazine article, if it were not also an aesthetic experience. Anyone who cares to examine my work will see that even when it is downright propaganda it contains much that a full-time politician would consider irrelevant. I am not able, and I do not want, completely to abandon the world-view that I acquired in childhood. So long as I remain alive and well I shall continue to feel strongly about prose style, to love the surface of the earth, and to take pleasure in solid objects and scraps of useless information. It is no use trying to suppress that side of myself. The job is to reconcile my ingrained likes and dislikes with the essentially public, non-individual activities that this age forces on all of us.

It is not easy. It raises problems of construction and of language, and it raises in a new way the problem of truthfulness. Let me give just one example of the cruder kind of difficulty that arises. My book about the Spanish Civil War, *Homage to Catalonia*, is, of course, a frankly political book, but in the main it is written with a certain detachment and regard for form. I did try very hard in it to tell the whole truth without violating my literary instincts. But among other things it contains a long chapter full of newspaper quotations and the like, defending the Trotskyists who were accused of plotting with Franco. Clearly such a chapter, which after a year or two would lose its interest for any ordinary reader, must ruin the book. A critic whom I respect read me a lecture about it. 'Why did you put in all that stuff?' he said. 'You've turned what might have been a good book into journalism.' I happened to know, what very few people in England had been allowed to know, that innocent men were being falsely accused. If I had not been angry about that I should never have written the book.

In one form or another this problem comes up again. The problem of language is subtler and would take too long to discuss. I will only say that of late years I have tried to write less picturesquely and more exactly. In any case I find that by the time you have perfected any style of writing, you have always outgrown it. *Animal Farm* was the first book in which I tried, with full consciousness of what I was doing, to fuse political purpose and artistic purpose into one whole. I have not written a novel for seven years, but I hope to write another fairly soon. It is bound to be a failure, every book is a failure, but I do know with some clarity what kind of book I want to write.

Looking back through the last page or two, I see that I have made it appear as though my motives in writing were wholly public-spirited. I don't want to leave that as the final impression. All writers are vain, selfish, and lazy, and at the very bottom of their motives there lies a mystery. Writing a book is a horrible, exhausting struggle, like a long bout of some painful illness. One would never undertake such a thing if one were not driven on by some demon whom one can neither resist nor understand. For all one knows that demon is simply the same instinct that makes a baby squall for attention. And yet it is also true that one can write nothing readable unless one constantly struggles to efface one's own personality. Good prose is like a window pane. I cannot say with certainty which of my motives are the strongest, but I know which of them deserve to be followed. And looking back through my work, I see that it is invariably where I lacked a *political* purpose that I wrote lifeless books and was betrayed into purple passages, sentences without meaning, decorative adjectives and humbug generally.

1947

Some other Penguin books by George Orwell
are described on the following pages

Other Penguins by George Orwell

ANIMAL FARM

In this biting satire upon dictatorship George Orwell, who has been compared to Swift, tells the story of a revolution that went wrong. The animals on a farm, led by the pigs, drive out their master and take over the farm. But the purity of their original doctrine is soon perverted.

'A very amusing and intrinsically wise book' – *Guardian*

NINETEEN EIGHTY-FOUR

1984 is the year in which it happens. The world is divided into three great powers, Oceania, Eurasia, and Eastasia, each perpetually at war with one another. Throughout Oceania 'The Party' rules through the agency of all-powerful ministries. The authorities use every device to keep a check on the people's thoughts, words, and deeds. Against this nightmare background is played out the drama of Winston Smith, who rebelled against the Party's rule.

Inside the Whale and Other Essays
George Orwell

The essays in this book, literary, political, or descriptive of
experience, are typical of George Orwell and his role as the
conscience of our age. From *Down The Mine*, a description of
Orwell's visit to a coal mine which brings home to us in his
vivid prose the effort and horror of a miner's work, to *Politics
and the English Language*, where his own crisp exact use of
English as much as his actual words gives point to his plea for
a meaningful use of language, and *Boys' Weeklies*, a carefully
presented and thorough piece of research, they bear out the
remarks of *Time* –' . . . there are no replacements for a George
Orwell, just as there are no replacements for a Bernard Shaw
or a Mark Twain. . . . In his literary criticism and his political
essays he pricked, provoked, and badgered lazy minds,
delighted those who enjoyed watching an original intelligence
at work.'

Also available

COMING UP FOR AIR · HOMAGE TO CATALONIA

KEEP THE ASPIDISTRA FLYING

DOWN AND OUT IN PARIS AND LONDON

THE CLERGYMAN'S DAUGHTER

*For a complete list of books available please write to Penguin Books
whose address can be found on the back of the title page*